Out of the Dark Into the Sun

To Faye

Best Wishes
Linda Givans

Linda Givans

BEARHEAD PUBLISHING
- BhP -
Brandenburg, Kentucky

BEARHEADPUBLISHING
- BhP -
Brandenburg, Kentucky
www.bearheadpublishing.com

Out of the Dark
Into the Sun
by Linda Givans

Cover Design by Bearhead Publishing
Photo Photography by April True
Graduate from Male High, Louisville, KY

First Printing - November 2014

ISBN: 978-1-937508-33-3
1 2 3 4 5 6 7 8 9

Disclaimer

This book is a work of fiction. The characters, names, places, and incidents are used fictitiously and are a product of the author's imagination. Any resemblance of actual persons, living or dead is entirely coincidental.

Proudly printed in the United States of America.

Out of the Dark Into the Sun

Follow me on Facebook at:
Linda Givans Author Page

Dedication

Book will be dedicated to my husband Larry for his patience.
And to my six grandchildren, April, Kelsey, Julia,
Justin, Kaylei and Waylon.

My prayers go to all families that have lost a child to abuse or
abduction and pray for their safe return.

Chapter One

My name is Sophie Lawson. My hometown of Garrett, Kentucky has only a few small businesses. One of these businesses is an auto repair shop and gas station that my dad owns, another is the only bank in town where my mom works.

Even though today is Saturday, mom and dad are at work. A senior in high school, I am more than old enough to live by myself, but due to finances I continue to live at home with my parents. After graduation I plan to go to college if I am accepted, I want to study law and move to New York City My best friend Nicky, whom I've known since kindergarten, plans to go to the same college.

My job today is to clean the house. I have no plans afterward. Just as the thought occurs to me that I might phone Nicky, the phone rings.

Listening to Nicky's familiar, high-pitched voice, I could hear her say. "Sophie, some of us are meeting tonight at the Towne Mall to check out the local guys. What do you say? Can you get your mom's car tonight?"

We have a few hangouts for the younger generation nearby, in Elizabethtown, the Towne Mall is one of these places. A lot of our class meets there on the weekends to have somewhere to go. I quickly reply to Nicky's questions, telling her, "I'll call mom at work. I'll call you back after I find out if I can get the car. Talk to you later."

"Okay, bye," she says.

I hang up the phone and get to the task of vacuuming the floor. After I finish, I call mom but the phone is busy, so I realize I will have to phone her later. Freedom, our fat lazy cat, lies all stretched out on the window sill. The morning sun flows freely through the window, making his black and white coat look very bright and clean. Very content with the warmth of the sun, he begins to roll and purr, rolling and rolling until he descends from the window sill. His large paws hit the hardwood floors with a thud. I guess Freedom is a good name for him; he has his own door that allows him to go at his own will. Sometimes he stays out all night. Thank goodness he's fixed.

Looking out the window, I can see the Wilsons getting in their blue Chevy van to go shopping or something. Mr. Wilson often talks to dad about cars and they both like to go golfing. Next to them lives a family with two small boys. We don't know them; they had just moved to the area. The boys play on their bikes. A pretty good neighborhood, we have lived here all of my life, as have many of the other occupants.

Thirsty, I turn and head for the kitchen. Getting a coke out of the refrigerator, I hear the phone ringing in the other room. Running down the hall to get the phone, I hit my toe on the edge of the wall. Pain shoots all across my foot. Hopping and gritting my teeth to keep from cursing,or crying out, I snatch up the phone. It's mom.

"Sophie," I hear her say. "I have to stop by the store but I won't be much later than usual."

My foot is still hurting a little but there's no blood, so I feel it will be okay. "Mom," I say and then repeat, "Mom" a little more loudly, so she does not hang up before I ask her about the car. "I was wondering if I could use the car tonight? Nicky and I want to go to the mall. I may find something to wear to the concert, you know our concert at school is next week."

After a moment, I hear mom's voice again. She says, "Maybe.... if you are not out too late"

"Okay, Mom. Thanks. We'll be home early, I promise," I assure her. Mom very rarely says 'yes' right away. Usually, she has to think about it for a while. It isn't that she doesn't trust me. This is merely her way of letting me know she is the mom and until I am an adult she is the one that has control. She always tells me I will understand when I have children of my own.

I go to my room to find my cell phone, I text Nicky to let her know that I will pick her up at six, I ask her what she'll be wearing tonight. I want to pick something similar. You never know who we might meet.

Nicky isn't sure what she's going to wear so I will have to pick out something on my own. After looking for a while, I decide on jeans and a pretty, green, lightweight sweater, I have a funky looking hat that goes great with the sweater. I will wear my hair down. It comes to my shoulders and is dark brown like mom's hair.

Mom makes it home about five thirty. I quickly exchange a kiss with her and took her car keys. "See you later, Mom," I say as I leave the house.

Before I'm able to fully escape, she calls after me, "Don't be late."

I continue as if not to hear her. Shutting the door, and dashing down the sidewalk, I jump into her car. It is a 2012 Chevy. Dad is going to buy mom a new car.

I tune the radio to my favorite station, which is country. I love singing along to my favorite songs. And off to pick up Nicky I go.

Since Nicky's mom and dad divorced last year, she and her mom live in an apartment on Column Drive. Nicky gets depressed if you talk about her dad very much so we don't mention him unless she brings him up first. As I pull into the parking lot, I can see Nicky coming down the concrete steps outside of the building facing the parking lot. She's waving; she's wearing a short, leather, black skirt and a white sweater, showing a small tattoo on her arm. She also is wearing her hair down with a headband across her head. She has a couple of hoop earrings on. I guess we look pretty cool - me with my funky hat and her with her leather skirt.

"Hello, girl, how are you doing?" She asks with a smile, as she hops into the car. "We are going to have a good time tonight."

"Nicky," I say, telling her, "You look great."

She replies, "Take a look at yourself, girl. We'll knock them out tonight."

Nicky flips the radio over to the rock station and begins to move, snapping her fingers like she's right out of a hard rock band or something. I've always known she's a little more hip than me. She always likes dressing a little loud and she has several tattoos on her arms and a belly button ring. My mom would never agree if I wanted to have any of this. But Nicky is always nice to me. My mom likes her and her mom.

As I pull into the parking lot in front of the mall, Nicky yells, "Sophie, look over there." Pointing, she asks, "Do you know whose car that is?" Before I have time to answer, she replies, "Sean Bentley." She knows I had a huge crush on Sean a couple of years ago. "You know how dreamy he always was," she reminds me, with that conniving little grin.

I open my car door and get out and Nicky follows suit. We hightail it across the parking lot and to the entrance doors to the mall. Inside, we walk for a while, checking out all the clothing stores. I see several dresses that I like. Then I spy one that I think would be perfect for the concert at school, a mint green with a little jacket. I try it on and it fits great, so I decide to get it. I have enough money, from a few odd jobs that I have done, to pay for it. Nicky is over by the jewelry, and she wants to know if I bought the dress. I hold the shopping bag up for her to see.

As we continue to walk around, all at once, in front of us, we see Sean and a friend coming from the opposite direction. Nicky punches me on the arm, so I know she's going to say something to him as they get nearer to us.

Sean is still very handsome. His thick, dark hair is even longer, and begs for fingers to be run though it; his eyes are dark brown and mysterious; and he stands about six-foot-two, with broad shoulders, showing he probably works out often. Soft spoken and clean dressed, he was one of the smarter guys in our class, I hated when he moved to another school. As he gets closer, I can feel my heart beat a little faster. Beside Sean is another boy I do not recognize. He is shorter and has reddish blond hair; he is wearing jeans and a tee shirt. He's not as good looking as Sean.

Drawing closer, Sean sees me and calls out, "Hey, Sophie, where have you been? I haven't seen you for a while."

I reply, nervously, "I...I've been around, just busy I guess."

He looks at his friend, saying, "This is my friend Rick. You and Nicky want to hang out with us for a while? We were going to "Motion Out" to check out the videos and movies, and maybe get something to eat afterwards."

Nicky pulls on my arm. "Sophie, we could do that for a while," she says.

I gently pull my arm away then agree to go with them. Sean says if we ride with them that he will bring us back to the mall after we finish eating so I agree.

So off we go with the guys. In the parking lot, I get in the front seat next to Sean, and Nicky cannot wait to slide in the back seat next to Rick. We decide we are hungry so the guys take us to a small burger shop on the way to the video store. Sean's car is a jeep, open top very airy and a rough ride but at least it's clean. After we get a table at the burger shop, Nicky and Rick disappear after only a few minutes.

After a while, when Nicky and Rick do not return, I become worried. "Sean," I say, asking, "Where do you think they have gone?"

Sean replies in a calm voice, "I'm sure they'll be back in a while." But his eyes, looking out the window and sweeping the parking lot, convey his concern as well.

We continue to sit there and talk about school, and I tell him that I plan to go to college in New York to study law. Sean says he is not sure what he's going to do. "My father wants me to take over his business some day," he shares, with an unenthusiastic shrug, and a stare in his eyes as evidence of his disapproval. His father has a bakery.

After waiting for a while longer, I glance at my watch and decide I need to go back to the mall, so I won't be late getting home. I motion to our waitress.

"Yes, honey," she says as she comes to our table.

"We need to leave," I tell her. "But another couple came here with us...."

"Yeah, I saw them," I'm relieved to hear her say.

"We're not sure where they've gone," I also share. I wait, and hope to hear her say that she saw where they went, but she says nothing. So I continue, "If either of them comes back looking for us, can we give you our cell phone numbers, so they can call us?"

"Sure," she says, nodding her head. "I'll be happy to help."

I'm not sure if it's my imagination or not, but I think the waitress' eyes look a little worried now as well.

"Thanks," Sean chimes in, as he hands her a few dollars tip and slides out of the booth.

Once I'm settled in his car, I call my mom and explain what's happened.

"What do mean Nicky's missing?" I hear her ask with alarm in her voice.

There's silence for a while, then I try to explain, "I don't know where she's gone Mom. She just disappeared with some guy.

"Okay," she says, and I can tell she's trying to gather her calm. "Get home, and pick me up. We need to go over to Nicky's apartment to tell her mom what's happened."

"I'll be there soon," I tell her.

"Be careful," she says, "and do"t forget I love you."

The words have more meaning right now than they usually do. My mom's and dad's love mean everything to me. They have always been my support.

As Sean drives me back to the mall, all I can think about is I really don't know Rick, and Sean doesn't know him that well either. Rick had just started at the school where Sean goes. The burger I've eaten just a short while ago doesn't seem to be settling too well in my stomach. I wish more than anything that my cell phone will ring and Nicky will say she's okay and ask for us to come back to the burger place and pick her up, but my phone remains silent, as does the conversation in the car between Sean and me.

I began to feel tears flow freely down my face as I wonder just what I am going to say to Nicky's mother. I kind of feel responsible for Nicky, since she was with me. If only Nicky and Rick had just stayed with Sean and me.

Chapter Two

When I get home to pick mom up, she comes around to the driver's side and says, "I'll drive."

So, with relief, I get out and walk around to the passenger side and get back in. A second later, we race off to Nicky's apartment.

"Mom," I say. "I am so worried about Nicky. I don't know why she and Rick left."

Mom replies, "It's not your fault. You are not responsible for what Nicky does."

Silence reigns the rest of the trip. As we pull in the parking lot of Nicky's apartment, we can see Nicky's mom standing on the balcony, a frail statue of a woman with some signs of graying noted at each temple. She looks very worried. She also looks like she has been crying.

Parking, getting out of the car, and climbing the stairs to Nicky's apartment, Mom takes Nicky's mom's small hand as she opens the door. "Have you phoned her?" She asks.

"Yes," her mom replies, nodding. I figure from her sad-eyed response that Nicky still is not answering her phone, even for her Mom. "We will have to wait for twenty four hours before the police will consider her as missing." Nicky's Mother also shares.

We stay the night there but Nicky does not phone. We decide to return home, but we do file a report with the police department. The next few days are awful. All I can think about is Nicky. *Where could she be?* I phone Sean but he says Rick has not returned to school either. Graduation is coming and I wonder where Nicky is and will she miss her graduation.

It has been a month since Nicky's disappearance, graduation day is finally here. But it just does not seem the happy day that I had anticipated. Standing in our blue gowns and tasseled hats, we all look very important, but it just doesn't seem important. Afterwards, Mom has a party at home and all our family is there. Even with all of this, I still don't feel happy.

I did receive a letter of acceptance from the college I chose in New York. I have a lot of planning to do to get ready for my transition to go to college. Mom and Dad have saved enough money to pay for the first year's tuition. I have started packing for college, but I'm not sure I can get it all in my car. As if he knows some changes are about to happen, fat cat Freedom slowly walks behind me in and out of my room.

As the day gets closer, looking around my room, I realize I am going to miss everything in here, all of my pictures hanging on the walls of my friends, the big stuffed pillow my grandmother had made for my room. I will miss that fat cat Freedom also. All I can do for Nicky is keep her in my prayers each day. Hopefully she's alright wherever she may be.

Mom, Dad and I always go to church together on Sunday. Several of our neighbors also attend the same church. Dad always reminds me that is the least we can do to be thankful for everything that we have. I want to continue this in New York. I don't want to forget my religion, ever. We attend the Catholic Church in Brandenburg, a small town close to us. For several weeks, Masses have been said for Nicky and her family.

I have talked to Nicky's mom several times. And I saw where both Nicky and Rick were listed as missing on the news. News reports say they have been kidnapped or something. I'm praying they will find them alive. I know that on the main road coming into our town a lot of large trucks travel.

I have tried several times to phone Nicky, hoping that just maybe she will pick up, but I never have any luck. They had a story about Nicky at school for all the students to see to help all the ones that were close to her cope with the fact she had not been found yet.

Nicky's Mom and Dad have gotten back together. They both were devastated because she was missing. I thought about how much this would make Nicky happy if she only knew. Actually, they have renewed their vows in the church. Our family had attended the service.

Mom and Dad drive to New York with me to check out the dorms and take some of my things since it all would not fit in my car. The buildings are large and gray in color, cold, and have scary looking large windows in the front. A large walkway leads up to the double wooden doors of every building. I knew this would be very different than high school. I think this is going to be a lot of hard work and several years of study but I know this is what I want to do. Grandma always said sticking to something until you reach your goal pays off.

We drive back home. School will start the next week, so I will get my car and the rest of my things and head out on my own. Dad makes sure my car is in good running order for the trip and tells me all of the do's and don'ts when traveling by yourself. I'm nervous but ready for my independence. I know mom is glad I'm taking her old car. She's excited dad's going to buy her a new car. She has picked out a new Mustang, something she always wanted.

When the day arrives to leave for college, the weather is perfect for the trip, with the sun brightly shining and birds singing their songs. Mom and Dad stand there with Freedom beside them. What a picture, everything that I love is here in this picture, and they are all waiting for a transformed young girl - a grown up - to return home with a law degree. I have all my directions laid out and I am ready to go. So after a few hugs and kisses, I climb in the car, wave goodbye, fight a few tears, and head on down the road, for the adventure of my life.

Looking back, one last time, at our white house, the yard that Dad keeps manicured, the small porch with the swing, I often sit in, I realize this will be stored in my memories, when I become an older woman. Then I think, *the time for independence is now.* Leaving my childhood behind, I continue on my trip.

Chapter Three

As I drive farther from home, for the first time I feel like an adult, like I have my own life to figure out. I can be what I want to be. I have my own car, a room at the dorm, "This is the life". Also, there is some fear, but this eases as I remind myself that Mom and Dad are still there if I need them.

Dad has marked my map so I can go the right route, and reminded me to phone him each time I stop so he will know where I am at. After driving for about four hours, I decide to pull over and rest, maybe get something to eat and drink. A small diner is just ahead, looks like a fast food place. As I walk into the diner, I look around, There are a couple of teens and a man in one booth and a man who looks to be about twenty years old sitting alone at the bar.

The aroma of fresh cooked hamburgers fills the air, making me very hungry. I sit down in an empty booth. In a few minutes a heavyset lady, with red hair pulled back in a bun, a small tattoo at the side of her right arm, showing a dove with a flower in its mouth, comes over to take my order. Looking at me with a large smile, she says, "Hello, welcome to our diner. Can I get you a drink or something to eat?"

I could not help noticing she is clean and has on an apron over jeans and a tee shirt. The tee shirt reads "Big Roaster's Dinner". Very friendly, her cologne is a little overpowering, especially mingled with the smell of the hamburgers. I decide to get a soft drink and a grilled cheese.

While I'm waiting for my order, I look around the room again. The man at the bar is sipping on his coke. I notice his dark skin, and neatly trimmed, black hair. I conclude he's very nice looking. As I am looking at him, he turns to get up and he looks at me. I quickly turn around, but I continue to feel his dark eyes looking at me. I don't look back at him. I don't want to encourage anything, knowing that I'm traveling by myself. As music fills the air, "On A Pontoo", it reminds me how much I like this type of music. My food soon arrives and I eat my sandwich and drink my drink. I also phone dad to tell him where I'm at. After paying my check, I walk out of the restaurant, I'm cautious as I walk to my car and get back inside.

The rest of the drive is long and tiring. After several stops, I arrive at the dorm. As I check in, I find out that my roommate is a girl named Marsha Johnson, originally from West Virginia. She and her mom have moved to New York so she can attend this college.

Marsha is a tall girl with red hair. Pretty and very friendly, she's eager to show me around. She's been here several days already. She's very funny and always making me laugh. As we start classes, I notice she has her blouse on backward. I'm cracking up as I get her attention to tell her.

I soon find that classes are very hard and require a lot of reading. Not a lot of time to phone Mom and Dad, I call when I can, but most of the time I'm very tired. Looking back at high school, I realize it was a lot easier than college.

One day when Marsha and I stop by the local sub shop to have lunch, I notice a sign in the window saying, 'Part time help needed'. I decide to apply. I could use a little extra money. All the employees wear black pants and a white shirt. Most everyone that works here is from the college. The manager is most likely in his twenties. He's soft spoken and very friendly. He tells he needs someone to work in the evenings. I get the job and will start next week.

Having the job will help so I don't have to ask my parents for extra money. I soon find working at the sub shop is a lot of fun. Everyone is friendly, and I get to meet a lot of the students from college, some that aren't in my classes. This one group always comes in together, four girls and a couple of guys. They seem preppy, always dressed in expensive looking clothes, the current styles in everything. I believe one guy is named Barth. He looks in my direction once in a while, but he doesn't talk much, usually just places his order.

Marsha knows that I think he is very cute because I often speak of him. For some reason, she warns me to stay clear of him. She says he's nothing but trouble, mean, and impolite. I just can't see this. Barth is always nice to me. Every day continues to be busy for me, but I'm making pretty good grades, I have to keep up my study time in order to pass the classes though.

I usually work Tuesdays, Thursdays, and the weekends. Today is Saturday, no school, but I have to work. I have been working a couple of hours. I look out the window and I see Barth and a couple of those rich chicks walking up the sidewalk to front of the shop. As they enter, I hear one of the girls say, "Hey Barth, that waitress is here, the one you think is so cute. Why don't you ask her out?" She giggles as she asks. Thinking that I was not be the type of girl he would ever be interested in, I quickly look in the other direction. I could not imagine, not for a minute, that they could be talking about me.

When I turn around, Barth is standing at the counter. The girls have sat down in a booth. They then continue their conversation, with whatever other gossip they could discuss. Barth is standing right in front of me. I can feel a sweat break out across my forehead.

"Hello," he says. His voice is deep and soft.

I feel like melting, right in the spot I am standing. "I have seen you at college. I don't know your name. How do you like it here?" I reply, looking into his dark eyes. "I like it ok. It is hard, but I'm making it alright. How about you" I ask as I smile back at him.

"I'm doing okay too," He tells me, as he smiles back, showing nice white teeth. "I'm Barth Cummings, by the way," he says, then dares to ask, "And you are'"

"I'm Sophie. Sophie Lawson," I reply.

"Nice to meet you, Sophie. So what are you studying at Columbia University?"

"I'm studying Law. I always was interested in law," I answer.

"My father and brother are New York policemen, so I'll probably follow in their footsteps or I am really interested in working with the F.B.I. and the police department. Who knows," he shared with a shrug.

As we stand there finally talking with one another, it's like I'm hypnotized, or something. I don't think this is a feeling I have experienced before. Barth has dark brown hair; he's thin and tall - about six foot two inches. He has muscles on his arms and shoulders, like he's been working out. His eyes are dark brown and make me feel very warm when I look into them, like I am now. All of the sudden, out of the blue, I recall Sean and realize Barth and Sean do look similar. This turns my happy, warm moment to sadness, as I realize I have not heard from Sean since Nicky's and Rick's disappearance. Sensing a change in my mood and noticing the conversation has grinded to a halt, Barth gives me his order and heads off to the booth with the girls he had come in with.

When his order comes up and I take it to him, he says, "Sophie, I have an extra ticket to an Eagles concert next Friday night. Would you be interested in going with me?"

I just stand there for a while, hearing Marsha's voice in my head saying, 'Stay clear of him' but I want to go. So I finally say, "Yeah, I'd like to go with you"

"So where do I pick you up?" He asks with twinkling eyes.

I tell him what dorm I'm in and my room number. Then I walk away and leave him with his friends again.

Is this true? Am I really going to a concert next Friday night with Barth? I ask myself, hardly able to believe it. But I know that he has really asked me and I've really said yes. I feel very happy about this decision.

Later, I take the check out to Barth's table. As he pays the bill and gets up to leave with his friends, he tells me, "I'll see you Friday night at six o'clock, Sophie"

I merely smile, nod and wave goodbye. I'm so excited but I don't know how I'm going to tell Marsha. I keep telling myself she will understand. After all, just because she doesn't like Barth doesn't mean I shouldn't.

Chapter Four

The next few days, I keep very busy. Between school and the job and all of the studying, research and reports to prepare, there isn't a lot of time left. I have not discussed the fact that I have a date with Barth this Friday with my roommate. I just don't want to hear her response.

On my way to work, I can hear my cell phone ringing. Scrambling to get it out of my purse, I drop it to the floor of my car. It stops ringing.

Once I get to the place where I can pick it up, I notice the number indicates Barth has called. I call him back. I hear Barth's voice say, "Hi, Sophie, I was just verifying our date Friday night is it still on?" We talk for a while and we are all set for the date.

I think I might tell Marsha tonight because we are scheduled to study on our reports together then. Marsha comes home and we have a bite to eat. I begin to tell her about Barth, "Hey, Marsha, I saw Barth the other day and he asked me to go to a concert this Friday. I agreed to go. He seemed polite and I just thought I would go."

Quiet for a while, Marsha finally turns and stares at me with eyes that look as if she could kill me. Then she shouts, "Are you nuts? He's the worst person for anyone to go out with. You just don't understand!" And she runs off into her bedroom.

I try to get her to explain but she doesn't want to talk about it. Today is Thursday. I don't understand Marsha's attitude about Barth but I decide to phone him and cancel the date. For the next several weeks I don't hear from Barth. I wonder how he is doing but I realize he most likely thinks I'm not interested in him since I have canceled our date. I want to call him but Marsha will not let it alone. She continues to remind me what an awful person she thinks he is.

Marsha grows farther, and farther, away. She's constantly missing classes at college and her grades are falling. I want to help her but she will not let me. She says she doesn't need any help. So I finally decide to go on with my own life. She comes by one day and says she's going to quit college and she moves out from the dorm.

I continue working at the sub shop, and once I see Barth again but he never asks me out again. One day one of the teachers at college tells me about a job working with Mr. Finch. He's a lawyer, and works a lot of criminal cases. My teacher thinks it will be a great experience for me. I am excited. This is what I always wanted to do. I have been in college for some time now but still have a while before I will graduate.

I decide to wear a ladies' navy blue suit for the interview with Mr. Finch. I hurry so I will not be late. It's raining today and the traffic is terrible. Horns blow and pedestrians run across the streets trying to get to their destinations, putting their lives in their hands. Finally, I see the parking garage and pull in, hoping to find a vacant parking spot.

I leave the garage and find the elevators. I have a piece of paper in my pocket with the office number on it. His office is on the tenth floor. I hate elevators, but am not sure I could make it walking up ten floors without being out of breath. As soon as I exit the elevator, in front of me is a large wooden door with glass at the top. It reads Lawyers, Baker And Finch, Suite 1025, DuPont Sq.

I tell his receptionist, a middle-aged woman with blonde hair, wearing a dress skirt and a white blouse, very professional looking, I have an appointment with Mr. Finch.

"Mr. Finch, I Have a Miss Sophie Lawson in the office to see you," she says as she picks the phone up to inform Mr. Finch that I am here. "Please have a seat over there. He will be with you shortly," she tells.

After a few minutes, after getting a call from Mr. Finch, she says I can go in to speak with him.

When I walk into the office, I can see other offices off to the side with people walking around with papers. Some are on computers, some are talking on the phones. But just in front of me, Mr. Finch is sitting at his desk. He's an older man. His hair's neatly cut and grey on the side. He also has a thick, grey mustache. He's looking over his wire-framed glasses at me, in his dark grey business suit.

I hold out my hand and introduce myself. "I'm Sophie Lawson. I have an appointment with you." I tell him.

He replies with a smile, "Yes, I believe you do. So you are studying law"

I explain that the law always interested me, even as a child. I used to play like I was a judge. After talking to me for a while, he gets up from his desk and begins walking me around and introducing me to the other people in the office. He tells me I'll be working with another girl in the office. Her name is Gail, and she has been with the firm for many years. Gail looks to be about thirty five years old and tells me she has two children. She also shares that there are a lot of papers that need to be composed and filing to be done. In other words, I will be busy.

I'm hired and soon find that working at the law office is great. I learn a lot and am able to sit in on a lot of cases. I keep my interest in everything about the law. At times, I don't agree with the way some of the cases end, but I usually just keep my mouth shut.

After work one day, I think I might go to some of the shops before going back to the dorm. As I'm on my way back to the parking garage, I see two women and a small child getting on the bus. As they step up to board, I catch a glimpse of Marsha and I guess, her mother. I have never met her mother, and I haven't a clue who the child is, maybe she's babysitting or something. I run to say hello, but she quickly gets onto the bus and does not speak to me. I'm not sure why she doesn't want to speak to me.

Graduation day will be here soon and Mom and Dad plan to be here for the special day. Barth will be graduating also. I am excited to graduate, but I know that the boards will follow and I need to pass the Boards before I can have my own practice. Working under Mr. Finch will help me to get started on my own also. I believe that it is a requirement, to work under another lawyer before you can start your own practice as a lawyer.

On our big day, I'm nervous. As Mom and Dad sit in the audience, I can see how proud they are of me. I am happy to have such loving parents. Barth Cummings is one of the first people called to the stage to accept his diploma. Barth took Forensics, and criminal aspects, in college. He graduates with honors. Working with the N.Y.P.D. and the F.B.I. is his dream. Being a Lawyer, and having him as my boyfriend is mine. After the graduation, I see him and some of his family pass by. He looks in our direction and speaks as they make their way through the crowd.

My parents and I go out for dinner that evening. They spend the night in a motel, having to leave to go back home tomorrow. Their plane leaves early.

After working in the law office for about a year, Mr. Finch asks me if I would want to sit in on an interrogation of a man they had picked up they think is involved in a child abduction case. It has been all over the news that a small girl is missing in our area. The family has posted on the news begging anyone with any information to please come forward. I think about it for a while and decide that I want to do the sit in.

I moved out of the dorm and now have my own apartment. I also got lonesome for the fat cat from home named Freedom, so I bought a small grey and white kitten, who I name Donut. I wish I had all of her energy, she bounces around like a ball, swinging off my drapes every chance she gets. I named her Donut, because she will eat a box of powered donuts in a seconds. Donut also likes to sleep in my bed. Her little warm body and soft hair keep me warm and I feel like I have company.

Mr. Baker's, a lawyer who often works with Mr. Finch, is to pick me up to go to the interrogation tomorrow morning at nine o'clock. I can hardly sleep; all I can think about is that little girl and what the poor family must be going though. They have hired Mr. Baker to help them find their child. He has been on these kind of cases before. He has located some children, some children are never found. In addition to being a lawyer, Mr. Baker works with the F.B.I. as an investigator in child abductions. The missing child's family has offered a ransom for the return of the child. Goose bumps raise on my arms when I think what may have happened to the little girl, or where she is.

I take a warm shower, hoping this will help me relax enough to go to bed. Holding my head back, letting the warm water run down my back, I can feel my muscles begin to loosen up. Stepping from the shower, I wrap myself in a robe I have just taken from the dryer. The warmth feels so good. After that I fix a warm cup of tea and sit on the bed. Donut is eager to play a game, so I take a few minutes to play with her. There is a piece of yarn on the dresser; this is her favorite thing. After a short while, I lie on the bed and pull the cover over my legs, feeling myself give in to the night of sleep.

Out of the Dark Into the Sun

I am awakened by the sunlight shinning through the window in my bedroom, as my alarm starts going off. I quickly shut off the alarm and jump out of the bed. I look in my closet to find something to wear today. I go downstairs to the front entrance to wait for Mr. Baker.

The horn gives a little beep as Mr. Baker pulls over to the curb. I open his door and slip into the front seat. I look at him; he has a big smile. He asks, "Are you ready for this?"

I don't know how to answer him. I'm not sure if I'm ready or not. But finally, the words come out, "I just hope we get the truth out of him."

The rest of the trip we both remained silent.

As we walk into the room where we're to meet the prisoner, it's dark and feels cold and scary. A large table sits in the middle of the room, to the side two chairs for Mr. Baker and myself, on the other side, a single chair for the man to be interrogated.

Next thing I notice the door opens and an officer brings a man in handcuffs, and ankle chains in. The man is a tall, dark looking guy. He looks dirty and has several tattoos are showing on his arms. One, I notice right away, is an ugly snake looking like it is ready to strike anyone close to him. He's sitting in the chair.

Mr. Baker proceeds to tell him who we are. Next the questions and answers start. The man's name is Parker Brunner. They have found clothing that belonged to the child in a dumpster near his apartment. He has been arrested before for sexually abusing a child in his own family.

The man sits there denying that he had anything to do with the child's clothes. Then he asks, in a rough sounding voice, "Why do you jerks always try to pin all of this shit on me?"

Jumping from his chair, Mr. Baker pins the prisoner to the wall, with his arm under Parker's neck. In a snarl, he says, "Listen to me, you piece of trash! If the world had less people like you, maybe we would not have to worry about our children."

The officer rushes to help Mr. Baker. I just sit there as it all unfolds in front of me. After this, they take the prisoner out of the room.

As we settle in the car to return home, silence fills the car. Then finally Mr. Baker speaks, griping the steering wheel, with a angered look on his face, peering out the front window, and looking over my way every once and while. "I know that bastard is guilty. He is going to just walk right out of there and hurt another child. The police don't have enough evidence to hold him."

I don't answer for a while. Then all I can say is, "We have to get more evidence, we have to"

Mr. Baker replies with a grimace, "That is easier said than done."

I remember someone telling me that Mr. Baker had a daughter but she died from cancer. She was about the age of the missing child. I'm sure that this was heavy on his mind during the interrogation.

After returning home, I'm exhausted, so I eat something and play with Donut for a while. The haunting images of Brunner keep surfacing in my mind - long brown oily hair, dark circles around his eyes, in those jail clothes that mark the criminals, and that ugly tattoo of a snake on his arm. I could not see any signs of love or passion in that face. I watch television for a while. There isn't any show I'm interested in, so I decide to go to bed.

Mom phones me the next morning. While we're talking, she tells me that the local news said that two bodies have been found in the landfill in Louisville, Kentucky, but they have not been identified yet and the families have not been contacted. I'm hoping that it is not Nicky and Rick. They have not been located either. I just always tell myself that Nicky did not want to be found, and they just ran away together somewhere.

Time was getting closer for our trip to Cancun. Mr. Finch invited six people to go on the trip with him and his wife. There is a lawyers' convention going on during this time, I was one of the six he invited. I an getting more excited as the time passes. I have bought a few new clothes to take on the trip, I'm looking forward to warmer weather. Hoping for better weather I am sure to pack a bathing suit, and summer clothes.

We stay busy at the office, trying to get everything finished for the trip. My phone rings at work and I can see that it is Mom. I know something is wrong; she never calls me at work. When I pick up the phone, I know that something's terribly wrong by the sound in her voice. "Sophie, I have very bad news," she says. "The bodies... the bodies," she stutters. "They were Nicky, and Rick. They said they were beat to death, put in a large plastic bag and thrown into that landfill."

Cold chills ran through my entire body. *How awful!* I just cannot believe Nicky's life was gone in a blink of the eye. "Mom, what about the funeral?" I ask in a shaky voice.

"I don't know right now, Sophie. I'll call Nicky's Mom and then I'll let you know. Okay?"

"Yeah," I answer in a very low tone, trying not to cry on the phone. "I definitely want to go. I know Nicky's mom will need all the support she can get."

"I'm sure," Mom agrees. "Sorry to have to break the news to you, but I knew you'd want to know. Are you okay?"

"I'm upset, but I'm okay," I answer. "Just let me know about the funeral as soon as you find something out."

"I will," she promises. "Love you."

"Love you, too, Mom. Give Dad my love too," I say and end the call.

Gail comes in the office as I hang the phone up. Tears are running down my face. "Sophie, what's wrong?" She asks, grabbing a tissue from a box on a nearby table and handing it to me.

"Gail, it's my best friend from high school. She and a friend, they were... they were.... murdered!" I say, as the tears will not stop.

"Murdered. They were Murdered?!" Gail asks in disbelief.

"Yes," Mom just phoned. "She told me."

"That's awful. I'm so sorry. Sit down, I'm going to get you a glass of water," Gail says as she leaves the office for a few minutes. Returning with a bottle of water, she suggests, "Sophie, why don't you go home for the rest of the day. You, need time to recover from this awful thing."

"I think you are right," I reply, as I wipe the tears from my face.

I later find out that the funeral is in a couple of days, so I make plans to attend. I book a flight to Louisville and a return ticket for the next day. I'm uneasy about flying but I know I want to be there. The flight is not bad. The little lady I sit next to is very nice; she has flown several times. We talk though most of the flight.

When entering the airport, I can see Mom and Dad walking toward me. Mom still looks young to me even though she has just turned fifty two. She always dresses nice; she's wearing brown dress pants and a beige, lightweight sweater, with matching jewelry, and dress flats. Her hair is always styled. She usually wears it short with some curls on the top. She continues to wear some makeup each day. Dad usually, always wears the uniforms from work unless he's at church or at a funeral. He's fifty six, with a stocky build, and muscles on his shoulders and arms. As I walk up to them, they put their arms around me.

"Hello sweetheart, we are so glad to see you," Mom says with a bittersweet smile. We know this will not be easy for any of us.

Have you ever been to a funeral when it's not raining? I don't think I have. It continues to pour though the entire service. The service is at Saint John's Catholic Church in Brandenburg, Kentucky. Burial services are at the nearest Catholic graveyard. I feel bad for Nicky's Mom and Dad. Her father has to pull her mom away at the gravesite service after it is finished. There are about a hundred people at the funeral, different ones from church, family and friends. Some of the kids from school, and teachers also are there.

When I return to work, some of the people have bought me a pretty house plant, and a sympathy card. We do not talk much about the funeral. Everyone is trying to focus on our trip. I guess no one wanted to put a damper on the excitement of the trip. In other words, I guess life goes on and the people we lose along the way are only our memories.

Chapter Five

I didn't pack for the trip until about four o'clock. We are going to leave at six in the morning for the airport. I have also packed suntan lotion, a couple of beach towels, and sunglasses in a bag. I sit this on the floor beside the luggage. I look everywhere, but can't find Donut. I needed to find her, because the man in the next apartment said he would watch her while I was away. I look in the bathroom, and my bedroom. That cat is not to be found, so at the last minute, I decide to look in the bag on the floor. Two little ears shoot up. Little blue eyes peer at me, as if to say, 'Are we going somewhere?' Then her furry paw hits my hand to let me know she's not pleased that I'm going to leave her here.

Early the next morning, I manage to get all my luggage out to the front of the building, where I wait for the cab to take me to the airport. Here I will meet Mr. Finch and the rest of our group .Soon, I see the yellow cab turning the corner to pick me up, and off to the airport we go. The streets are busy as usual, but the cab driver doesn't seem to mind. I guess he's used to it. The sun has not come up yet and the air is quite cool. I'm wearing a coat, but can't wait to remove it when we get in a warmer area.

The cars are hurrying about all in a line for the airport. We slowly move up until it's my time to unload at the entrance. The cab driver's nice enough to help me with my luggage. I give him a little tip for the effort, and say, with a smile, "Thank you, sir."

Mr. and Mrs. Finch are standing in the lobby. We wait for a minute and the other people in our party meet us. We then rush to get to the right gate to load for our flight. They have gotten a lot stricter on how much luggage you can bring on a flight, so I was careful how much I brought. The flight attendant is very helpful to show us to our seating area. Gail and I are seated together. She's all smiles. "Hope you aren't too nervous," she said.

I look back at her and tell her I am broken in a little bit from the flight I took to Louisville. "Even though my thoughts on the flight were on Nicky's funeral and her parents, all the way to Louisville," I explain to Gail. She's quick to say she is going to order a drink to help with her nerves, thinking I probably need one also.

After we all settle in our seats and are instructed how to fasten our seatbelts and how to exit the plane if there is an emergency, we begin to taxi down the runway. Flying to me feels like kind of being in the belly of an enormous bird looking for the perfect place to make a nest, only he's looking for the tallest tree around to support his large body. As he picks his feet up to soar high, and higher into the blue sky, now he can take a breath again.

Soon as we level off and take that breath, the flight attendant is there to see if we want a beverage. Gail gets her drink and I settle for a diet coke. Mr. and Mrs. Finch are sitting across from us and it looks like they have some kind of a mixed drink.

As I sit next to the window, I can see the sun shining through the clouds. They are huge pieces of cotton so white that they hurt your eyes if you look too hard. A shadow forms across the cloud of another plane as it passes by. I imagine Barth looking back at me and waving as our paths cross.

As Gail passes me a small bag of peanuts, I am brought back to reality. She says, "A penny for your thoughts. What were you thinking of?"

I reply, "Oh just old memories." Then our conversation turns to her family and her children. The girls have stayed with her sister and her husband is working.

I let my eyes close for a while, then I'm awakened to the sound of the stewardess asking everyone to place their seatbelts on. We are landing in Houston, Texas to change planes. We have a short stop before continuing on our next flight. I walk over to a shop in the airport to purchase a magazine and accidentally bump into a man in the shop. When he turns to look at me, after I have told him that I am sorry, my mouth flies open; I', shocked, it's Barth!

"Sophie," he says, "Is that you?"

"Barth," I reply. "What are you doing in Texas?"

He tells me he's working for the F.B.I. and is on a case. I find out he's also on his way to Mexico. Stopping in Cancun for a couple of days. He probably sees the excitement in my eyes. My heart is beating so fast. I almost forget that I am going to Cancun with the people from my work.

We board the new plane. Barth sits a few seats from Gail and me. Gail talks all the way to Cancun. I am sure I answer her, but I can't remember anything we talk about. All I can think about is how funny it is that Barth has been on my mind, even before I knew he was there. I tell him that we are staying at The Royal Grand. Barth says he's going to see if he can get reservations there also, and cancel at the place he had intended to stay. "Maybe we can have lunch and talk about our jobs and what our plans are," he says.

Our plane finally lands in Cancun. The air is soft and warm, and the sky is a beautiful blue. Everyone's so happy to be in a warmer climate. We hurry to get on the shuttle to our resort. I don't see Barth. I hope he was able to get the reservations switched to the resort we are staying at. As I look to the right, I see a large sign advertising a store from our area back home. I can't believe that this place has stores like we have at home. This place looks like what I feel Heaven might look like.

There are a lot of Mexican people about, several children by themselves. It looks, as if they are selling small bracelets, or something. When we arrive at the resort, the door man comes out to assist us with our luggage, and we proceed to sign in. The front entrance is something right out of the movies, everything is made of marble. Over our heads is a beautiful drawing very high onto the vaulted ceiling. Large columns, also made of marble, are around a huge open room. Around the room are different areas where people are sitting and having drinks. The back of the room is opened, leading to the pool areas. You can see people running around in their bathing suits. Behind the pool areas is the ocean. The ocean keeps a constant breeze blowing, and the constant sounds of the ocean completely make you feel relaxed and at the perfect temperature. Seagulls fly over the ocean, swooping down every now and then, hoping to find something to eat.

Gail, and I have a room together. I'm amazed at the room's two large beds with six pillows each. Each pillow has a different softness. Everything from hard to very soft, they are there to please. The large showers are walk-in with water that sprays all around, and over to the side is a Jacuzzi. I have never been in such an elaborate place. I'm sure I must of died and gone to heaven. Everything that you need is here at the resort. Five star restaurants are everywhere, and plenty of shops. This is a girl's paradise.

As I'm sitting and dreaming about this place, I can hear my phone ringing. It is hidden down deep in my large purse. I have brought this purse along because I can carry a lot in it, but now there's a problem trying to get to the phone when I need it. I know I will have to switch purses if we go out.

When I finally answer the phone, Barth is on the other end. He tells me, "Sophie, I am sorry. I wasn't able to switch to the Royal but I will come over there and maybe we could have dinner or something. Is seven o'clock ok?"

"Yes," I reply. "That sounds great."

When I end the call, I turn to Gail and ask her if she can tell Mr. and Mrs. Finch that I have plans with a friend tonight for dinner. She says, "Sure that's ok."

"You won't believe this but the man I'm going to dinner with is someone I knew from school. How weird is that to run into him here?"

"That's wild," she replied.

I'm so excited I'm finally going to have that date with Barth. For some reason, I feel connected to him. He cannot be as bad as Marsha had said; she just didn't know him. He's too polite to be the monster that she portrayed. I know she must have formed her opinion from rumors she heard or something. I'm trying hard to convince myself I'm right.

I pick several outfits, not sure what I should wear. I want to look a little sexy, but I don't want to overdo it. I have brought several long loose skirts that look great with sandals, and an off-the-shoulder summer blouse, which looks a little sexy. It is made out of a soft material and is a sunny bright orange. It will look good with the right necklace. So I finally decide on this outfit.

I'm going to meet Barth in the main lobby at seven o'clock. I hurry to get to the elevator. There are several other couples on the elevator. One couple is an older couple; they seem happy and remind me of my own parents. I wish they could see this place; I know they have never had a vacation like this. The other couple, I overhear them say, are on their honeymoon.

As I get off of the elevator, I can see Barth waiting, in the sitting area. He has dress pants on and a short sleeve casual shirt, so

I feel I'm dressed appropriately. He looks so handsome sitting there, his sun-kissed skin shows off the muscles on his arms, his face is close shaven, and his hair neatly groomed. I always feel that his eyes make you feel warm all over, he always has a soft smell of a man's cologne, which makes you want to just kiss him all over. I told myself I needed to hide that feeling until maybe someday it might be the appropriate thing to do.

As I walk closer to him, he looks up and begins to walk in my direction. "Hello, Sophie. I was glad you agreed to have dinner with me," he says; then asks, "Where would you like to eat?"

I am not familiar with any of the restaurants, so I let him choose. We eat at an Italian diner. It is very nice. Barth orders a sweet-to-taste, white wine to go with the dinner. I have a great time. Afterward we decide to go for a walk on the beach just behind the resort. Everyone has been warned not to get too far away from the resort, especially at night.

As we walk along the beach, I take my sandals off so I can feel the warm, moist sand between my toes. Moonlight lights the sky. It shines across the waves as they come splashing to shore. In the distance you could hear seagulls as they fly around, Barth and I talked about school, and what we want to do with our lives. He says he really likes his job, working with the F.B.I. department of investigations. He has to travel different places, and he enjoys going to different areas. His trips are paid for by the department. He also is back in New York a lot, to work with cases at N.Y.P.D. He says he will continue to live in New York.

I enjoy our date. He is very interesting, good looking, and great company. I know I would like to see him again. I feel he enjoyed our date also. As we continue walking, the night air becomes a little cool. I feel his hand reach for my hand, and he says, "Sophie, I hope we can do this again. I would like to continue to see you."

We both have stopped walking at this point. Looking into his eyes, I agree that we should continue to see each other. Barth leans over and kisses me and I kiss him back.

After such a magical night, I cannot wait to tell Gail when I return to the room. She's watching television, but she says she and Mr. and Mrs. Finch had a nice dinner also; they had eaten at a steakhouse. Mr. Finch was his old self telling the jokes that we all had heard a million times but they were having a great time, even if Mr. Finch was all eyes when some of the girls in bathing suits passed by. Gail said Mrs. Finch is used to that. She realized none of the babes would have anything to do with the old nut. I share all of my excitement from my date with Barth, especially, the "kiss". My toes still felt tingly, when I speak of it. She's thrilled for me.

I see Barth a few more times while we are in Cancun. He says that he will phone after we get back to New York. I know he's very busy on the case he's working on; he didn't talk much about the case, because he is not supposed to talk about it. The F.B.I. is very strict about what you can tell someone else. I know this because of working in the law office.

33

Chapter Six

I don't have to go back to the office until tomorrow, so once I get to the apartment, I proceed to unpack. I need to do some laundry, and pick up Donut. I had left him with Mr. Joe; I never knew Joe's last name. He has told me to call him, Mr. Joe. He's a nice, older man, an African American that lives by himself. He very seldom has any visitors. He seems happy to have Donut's company. I cannot wait to see my little fur bundle. Mr. Joe always is dressed in jogging pants a tee shirt and a robe; he seems clean so I guess he takes the clothes off, washes them, and then dresses back in the same clothes.

I knock on his door. As the door opens, Mr. Joe is smiling at me. "Hello, Sophie. Did you have a good time?" He asks.

Donut runs out, making several movements around my leg, letting me know that she's relieved that I have returned home. Mr. Joe picks her up, rubbing her back. He hands her to me. I can see she's wishing she could stay with him. I finally answer his question, saying, "I had a great time." I thank him for watching my cat, and give him some money, which he reluctantly takes. I'm sure that he can use the extra cash.

When we make it back to our place, Donut and I lie across the bed. Her favorite toy, a ball of yarn, is tossed about here and there. Next, she decides to make a run up the curtains in the bedroom. I look up at her and I can see her hair standing up. The excitement shows in her blue eyes, as the grey and white hair stood up. If only she could talk. I don't know if she's excited to be home or is giving me a cussing for being gone so long. So I get her down from the curtains, and give her a big hug to let her know that I love her little hair ball self.

The next few days, we are very busy at the office trying to catch up on all of the work. I know each day it's not too soon for the clock to turn to the time when we are able to leave for home. We are all talking about how Parker Brunner was let go due to the lack of evidence on the case of the missing girl. The child has not been found; her parents continue to have hope that she will be found.

There are no new leads in the case of the missing child. The police feel sure if she is found it will be a body now. They say there is a window of time, if the person is not found within that window, the chance of finding them alive is much less. I'm hoping this will not be true this time. I know they have had several Masses at Saint Paul's Church for the family.

Barth has phoned me a couple of times. He says that he will not be home for a couple of weeks. He feels the case he's working on is close in being solved. I know it will be great when he returns. I'm looking forward to seeing him again. He promised to take me out for dinner again.

Today is Tuesday. I am going to get off early. I need to go by the grocery store. I have planned on having a couple of people from work over for dinner tonight. I'm going to fix something simple, like lasagna and a salad, and maybe have some red wine. Gail says she will come over and help. She has to pick up her children and drive them over to her mom's.

As I turn to go to the store, I realize I turned down the wrong street. Some of the buildings are empty, and they have graffiti all over the sides. There are a couple of very small stores; they look dark and suspicious. The type of businesses operating here are not recognizable. I see a couple of girls with very short skirts and a lot of makeup on, and they just seem to be standing or walking down the street. I see one car pull over and a man is talking to the girl. I realized at this point, she must be a prostitute.

I see a man walking very fast down the street. That man looks very familiar, the tattoo of that snake, I remembered. *Oh, that is... yes, that is ... Parker Brunner!* I find myself thinking. *What is he doing down this street.* I'm sure he's up to no good. I decide to park the car, and follow him for a while. I want to see where he's going. I 'm scared, as I walk down the street, but I just have to see what he is up to.

Forgetting about my dinner guests, I continue to pursue Brunner. He turns and looks back but I don't think he sees me. I duck into a door front for a second. Then I continue but I can't see him.

"Where'd he go?" I must have lost him. Then, I feel an arm around my waist, pulling me into a doorway, as I kick and try to bite the arm around my waist. Then I hear his voice. *That deep, rough, voice.* "You bitch, why are you flowering me?"

Before I have time to answer, I feel pain, across my face, as he hits me in the mouth, with his fist. He yells, "Answer me, you bitch!"

I think I will pass out, but I don't. Then, again he says, "You bitch, you can go with the rest of them!" Next he says, "I remember you. You're one of the lawyers, from the jail."

I just keep quiet. I'm scared shitless at this point and my mouth is bleeding.

He grabs a rope, which is lying on the floor. He proceeds to tie my hands behind my back. All I can think of is *why did I stop to follow him? I could be killed!* Then I think about what he has said. *What did he mean? You can go with the rest of them.*

Next, he places a piece of duct tape over my mouth and a blindfold over my eyes. I can hear him talking to another man who has a Spanish sounding ascent. They seem to be talking about taking a boat out of the country.

I keep thinking, *someone will find me! They will miss me! They will call the police!* But then I remember how long the missing small girl has been gone. I think, *I 'm going to die!* Here I am sitting against the wall, blindfolded, hands behind my back, with duct tape on my mouth. *What can I possibly do?*

As I sit on the floor everything's quiet for the moment. I cannot hear Parker or the other guy. I think they must of left the room. My shoe has fallen off, when Parker threw me to the floor after binding my mouth with duct tape, blindfolding, and tying my hands behind my back. I can feel dirt or something with my bare foot. I hear a small squeak, as something runs quickly across my leg. I frantically want to scream, as I decide, *Oh, shit! It's a damn rat!* I start jerking my legs around to scare the thing, so it won't return.

In the distance, I think I can hear voices. They don't sound like Parker Brunner or the other guy. They sound like a woman, and I think I can hear children crying. I'm not for sure if this is coming from outside or in this building. I'm afraid to move from the spot I'm in. I cannot see and I'm not sure when they might return. I feel sick to my stomach, from getting hit so many times. I can feel the swelling around my eyes, and mouth. Blood has run down my chin and neck. I wonder if I have any teeth left.

I hear footsteps, and then the two men are back into the room. "Why'd you bring that bitch in here?" The other man asks.

Parker is quick to reply, "What, to hell, is it to you? The bitch was following me. I decided to take her with the rest of them! Go get the damn van, let's load them all up. We have to leave tonight!"

The thoughts keep running through my mind, *will they ever find us? Will I ever see Barth again, or is this the way it all ends?* As I feel a large hand grab me under my arm, my body is quickly brought to a standing position. There are no words just a lot of pushing, and pulling. My body hurts all over. I don't think I will ever live though all of this.

After a few minutes, I feel myself being tossed into what seems to be a van. I'm shoved into the back. It is large and roomy. The smell of gasoline is strong. After a few more minutes, other people are brought into the van. The woman I've heard before, and several children, are loaded. The children are crying. I hear Parker yell out to the woman to keep the children quiet, "Give them some of the medicine I gave you!" He yells. "Keep those kids quiet!"

I know now Parker has to be involved in the disappearance of the little girl that is missing. *He's doing something with children,* I contemplate. The women, says to Parker, "These kids need something to eat. They are hungry. We have to feed them!"

"Just shut your mouth! They will have food on the boat. We will be there before long." Parker shouts back to her.

I wonder where we are going, who these children and the women are. What can they be doing with any of us? The trip continues, a very bumpy, and rough ride. The children are quiet, sleeping I guess, after they have been given medication.

After what I figure to be about an hour and a half, the van stops. We are unloaded. We are taken on a boat. I can tell by the rocking and the water smells. I'm led down some steps. It is a long distance to the bottom, so I figure the boat must be a large one. The children are starting to wake up. I can hear the women talking to them. "Honey, come in here. Let's go to the potty. I promise to get you something to eat soon," she is saying.

The other man that was with Brunner came into the room with some food for the children, I was so glad. I wasn't hungry, but my mouth was dry as cotton. I felt it was so sore I didn't know if I could drink or not. But if anyone offered me a drink I would sure try.

After this other man, who speaks English with a Mexican accent, leaves the room, I can hear footsteps getting closer to me. Feeling a touch to my bruised shoulder, the woman tells me to be quiet. "Don't speak. I have water," she says. After she loosens the duct tape from my mouth, she gives me a drink of water. She reapplies the duct tape, before I have time to speak to her.

Seems like we have been on the boat forever, but every now and then the woman gives me a drink of water and once she feeds me a piece of bread. I ask who she is, she puts her hand over my mouth. "Please be quiet," she says. "You have to do everything they ask of you, or they will kill you! I have to do the same. They have my child. I don't know where he is, but they grabbed us both. They told me if I did not help with watching these other children, they would kill me and my child."

When she removes her hand from my mouth, I dare to ask her again, in a whisper, what her name is.

She finally tells me, "My name is Monica Lowe." Then she shares more, "Me and my five year old son were shopping. We're from the New York area. They stole my car with us in it. That was a couple of weeks ago. I haven't seen him for several days." She pauses; then continues, "They are taking us to a place in Belize. It is a secluded area where the children cannot be found. They connect them with wealthy people who want to adopt the children and don't want to go on a waiting list. They pay lots of money for the children. They do not care where they come from as long as they are healthy."

We can hear one of the men coming so Monica stops speaking so they will not hear us and quickly replaces the duct tape onto my mouth again. "We are coming through Customs. Keep those kids quiet down here!" He yells.

I remember reading about Belize. I think it is close to Mexico. I don't remember anything about crimes in this area. I wonder if this was what Barth is investigating. The children are quiet. I suppose Monica has given them medication to make them sleep again. When the children are sleeping, Monica comes back over so we can talk again.

Loosening the duct tape again, Monica says, "I didn't ask you what your name is."

I had forgotten to tell her, because the man was returning as I thought about it. "My name is Sophie Lawson," I tell her now. "I live in New York. Currently I am studying law there and working in a law office. I was following Parker Brunner, when I got nabbed by the creep."

She proceeds to say the older children that they picked up are used for pornography taping, and they sell the tapes to sick pedophiles. She also says, "I overheard Brunner talking to one of the men about watching some of the tapes. He says he enjoyed the tape and would play it for them if they want to watch it." Monica also tells me, "They have drugs on the boat." She overheard that they would watch the tapes and do drugs for enjoyment.

We can feel the boat come to a stop. Parker comes down with us. Monica whispers that he has an automatic weapon, so we will not make any noise as the boat is checked through customs. We can hear the border Customs' guards from up above. Apparently this boat has been through many times before. They seemed friendly with the driver of the boat. They are talking in Spanish. I cannot understand everything they are saying.

Monica has kept me alive on water, bread and baby food. The children had the same food and some of the babies had formula that they drank from bottles. Monica says she is very worried about her little boy. His name is Rasean. She thinks he is somewhere on this boat also. She isn't sure who is with him. She says her child is small build and looks just like his father. Monica says her skin was dark, but the little boy is lighter skin also like his father. She continues, "My husband is in the service, and is out of the States. He doesn't know where we are. I haven't heard from him since the day we were abducted."

There's a noise of the boat running, again and the smell of oil in the air. Even though Monica is busy keeping the babies changed and dry, the boat still reeks of urine. The poor children are restless when they are awake, so she is instructed to keep them medicated enough to make them sleepy until the trip is over.

We stay on the boat what seems like days before we finally come to the place we are to get off. My face feels raw from the duct tape, and my eyes are bruised and swollen shut. My arms feel like they are contracted from being tied behind my back so long. But I keep telling myself, *I am still alive.*

Parker comes back to the area that we are in the boat. I can feel his hand on my arm. "Sweetheart, we're going to have to get you cleaned up. You certainly won't be worth much the way you look now," he says as he runs his nasty hand up and down my arm. The strong smell of cigarettes, body sweat, and just plain dirt, is right in my face. For a minute I think I will surely vomit.

I can hear him talking to Monica, "We will be getting you all off the boat in a couple of hours. I will bring your brat back down here but don't you try anything, or I will kill you both. You got that!"

Monica says, "Yes, oh please bring my baby to me, please!" And she begins to cry.

I want to hold her and comfort her but I can't.

It seems another few hours pass before the boat stops again. I can hear footsteps. A small voice can be heard, "Mommy! Mommy!"

Then I hear Monica scream, "Rasean! Rasean! Mommy is here!"

Parker is a creep, but he did keep his word to Monica. Monica said that Parker brought the child down the stairs and went back up. She says that she's going to get started preparing the children to get off the boat. "There are a couple of babies and four children ranging from four to six years in age," she tells me.

After a minute, something sounding like gunshots can be heard. The sound is up aboard the boat.

"Sophie!" Monica screams. "I am going to untie you. Something's going on up there. We need to make sure the children are safe!"

She quickly unties my hands. My lips burn as she pulls the duct tape from my mouth. She proceeds to remove the blindfold. My eyes burn as they adjust to the light, since I have been blindfolded so long.

The children are frightened. Some have begun to cry. We are trying to comfort them. One small little girl, holding tightly to my leg, and looking up at me, is crying, "Mommy. No, Mommy!"

I reach down to pick her up. Dirty blond hair and big blue eyes are looking at me. Two little hands tightly tie around my neck, as her head lies upon my chest.

"I won't let anyone hurt you ever again," I reassure her.

Parker comes running down the stairs. "They will not take me, I will kill you all!" He shouts.

He goes straight for Monica, not even noticing that I am untied. Monica fights back, screaming and biting him. He slaps her across the face. I look down on the floor and I see a piece of pipe. Sitting the child down, I quickly pick up the pipe. Wrapping my fingers tight around the piece of pipe, I pull it back as far as I possibly can and let Parker have it across the back of his head. Parker falls, to his knees, dropping his gun. Monica franticly picks up the gun. Pointing it toward Parker, she pulls the trigger. A loud sound shatters my ears and then a bullet hits him in the stomach. I don't think he's dead, but he's not trying to get up. I stand there with my mouth hanging open, not really believing that Monica just shot Parker. As she lowers the gun and I see her arms trembling, I walk over and take the gun from her. I don't want to see it go off again by accident.

The next thing we know a group of people come running down the stairs to the area where we are located. By the way they are dressed, with the F.B.I. all over their black vests, we can tell these people are with the F.B.I. I quickly lay the gun on the floor at my feet. One of the agents says, "We need to get you all out of here!"

Picking the little girl back up, I begin to follow the officer. Monica grabs onto her son with one hand and a baby with the other. The agents help with the rest of the children. The gunshots continue above. We have to follow the agents closely so we don't get in the line of fire. One of the F.B.I. agents stays below with Parker Brunner until help comes.

They lead us to a large helicopter, on the dock, where we all board as fast as we can. We all are very excited to be free again. We also are exhausted. The children are still frightened, but they are very quiet now. I look over at Monica. She is leaning over holding on to her little boy. She is a medium built, African American women, a strong looking figure. Her clothes are dirty and torn. Her hair is short. A bead of sweat runs down her forehead and tears of relief stream down her face. She cannot take her eyes off of her sweet little boy. His big brown eyes are looking back at his mom.

There is peace in his face knowing that his mom will take care of him.

I feel lucky that Monica is there. She has become my friend. I owe my life to her. The little girl continues to hold tight onto my hand. I wonder who her family is. I feel I never want to let her go. She feels like my child; I don't want her to ever be hurt again.

Blades swiftly circle the top of the helicopter, creating a beating sound, as dust from the air pressure stirs from the ground, until everyone loads. Then the big helicopter begins to lift into the air. We are informed by one of the officers that we are going to the hospital in Cancun to be checked for any injuries. The officer asks us are names, Monica tells them her son's name and her name.

"Sophie Lawson," I speak up.

One of the agents, sitting toward the front of the helicopter, turns around. He's holding one of the children. He yells, "Sophie... Sophie Lawson?"

My eyes brim with tears as I look up. My heart fills with joy. "Barth, oh, Barth," I say, seeing his face. I reach forward as far as I can reach as our hands touch. Both children we are holding are clinging on to us for life, but our hands manage to touch.

There is no time for explanations. Just relief that these kids and our lives have been saved. With Parker Brunner out of the picture and all the others caught at the boat, maybe they could locate the rest of the operation, and lock them all up. *These people need to be off the streets*. There are my thoughts as the helicopter soars through the sky.

Chapter Seven

We don't drive five minutes until we are at the airport. We hurry down to the line of people waiting to go through Customs to return to the States. Barth has passports for us, which they check. They are familiar with our faces, since the news has spoken about the shooting at the boat, the arrests, and the abducted children that were located.

The trip back home is long and tiring. We sleep through some of the trip. I tell Barth about my job and how I had set in on the interrogation of Parker. He tells me, "We were sure that he was guilty, but we did not have enough evidence to hold him."

"When I saw him that day, I just had to follow, to see what he was up to," I tell him.

Barth says, "I've been covering the child abduction case for a while. That's why I was in Cancun, and the lead took me to Belize. But the last person I expected to find there was you, Sophie."

As I feel a strong hand gently wrap around my hand, I return a look of pleasure and soft smile to let him know I'm pleased with the touch.

Barth is an investigator for the F.B.I. working with the N.Y.P.D. He says, "My father works with the police department.

He's the Chief of Police, also my only brother Steven works for the N.Y.P.D."

I have never met his family. I'm sure they are nice people, if they are anything like Barth.

As the plane comes to a landing, from the passenger window, I can see news station vans and trucks everywhere. I'm not prepared for this sight. Barth says, "Listen, Sophie, don't be alarmed. I will handle this. There will be a news conference later. They will just have to wait until then."

Police are everywhere, as we leave the airplane. The police welcome us back and the news media begin their questions. "Sophie, tell us what happened. How did Parker Brunner abduct you" "How many children were there?" "Were they all from the New York area?" "Is Parker dead?"

Barth walks up to one of the news media, and proceeds to give some kind of a statement. "There will be a statement later, Sophie and me are exhausted at this time, but there will be a statement later." Then the police officers lead us both away from the news media.

As I turn the corner toward the exit, I can see mom and dad walking toward me. Then we all break into a run toward each other. "Mom, Dad, I love you" I scream.

"We love you, honey. Thank God you are alright!" They say, then we all begin to cry and hold onto each other.

The connection I feel to Barth is indescribable. All I know is I could just kiss him. As we leave the airport for home, all I can think of is, *I hope it will not be long until we see each other again.* Barth says, "Bye, get some rest. I will call you."

Mom and Dad are staying in my apartment until I settle back in at home. I'm so happy to be home. I take the key out to unlock the door. I can hear small purring sounds from within the apartment.

When I open the door, I expect Donut to come running out the door. But instead she's nowhere to be found.

Calling out her name, "Donut! Where's my baby. Donut?" There's silence for a second, next that small, "Meow! Meow! Purr..Purr." And she runs out from behind the couch. She then makes several turns around my legs, as if to say "So where you been so long?" I lean over and pick her up, rub her head, and kiss her on her head. "Momma's home, baby. Momma's home." My coming home gift is a small lick on the back of my hand, reminding me of a small piece of damp sandpaper.

"Sophie," Mom says, "you go lie down. I will fix something for us to eat." Dad goes to the couch and turns on the television. I go to my bedroom to rest. I really don't want to hear the news, just not right at this moment. Donut follows me. She isn't taking any chance of me disappearing, again.

Donut's small body feels warm and comfortable next to me. My eyes feel heavy, as I become very relaxed at home again without the worries of the awful surroundings I have left. Now my thoughts go to the children, hoping they are happy and comfortable back in their homes. I think about little Calah; I want her to be happy back in her home. I guess I'm being a little selfish, but I also hope that she will remember me.

Mom and Dad stay with me for the next week. They want to make sure that I'm going to be okay. All of the people from work come by to visit. They are very glad I'm home and came back in one piece. Each day I feel a little stronger, and back to my old self.

Chapter Eight

The N.Y.P.D. and the F.B.I. plan a ceremony in which awards for bravery are to be given to Barth and the other officers that helped in the capture of the people involved in the abduction of the children. I am supposed to attend and Barth says, "Monica needs to be there also." There will be a dinner and a dance following the ceremony. He asks me to go with him. This is mostly for the officers and their families.

All of the families will probably be there with the children. I'm hoping that Calah, and her family, will be there. I can't wait to see her again. I had promised her that she could see Donut. I know she would be happy about that. I'm wondering if Monica's husband will make it home from the service.

But today I'm going to relax. I know it will not be long until I return to work. Donut will then be by herself again. Looking around the apartment, I know I need to replace a couple pieces of furniture. My couch is scratched from Donut's claws, and that drab color of brown needs to be a more colorful color. It had been given to me from one of the girls from school. One lamp needs a shade on it. I definitely need an area rug in front of the couch.

There's a ball of yarn on the couch. I gently give it a toss. As it rolls across the floor, Donut goes into attack mode. All I can see is the yarn wrapped with that silly kitten rolling from side to side. She seems very content that I'm back in her life. I also am content to be back in a safe haven.

The next few days I plan to go back to a regular routine of working. Everyone from the office is so helpful in updating me on everything that is going on there. We have taken on several new cases that I need updating on. I also find out that Parker Brunner has survived his shooting and is recovering in the hospital, before going to jail. I'm sure they have enough evidence to convict him this time.

Sliding the Mirror front doors to my closet, I take a look to see if I have something I feel will be nice enough to wear to the Awards Ceremony. I want to look great for Barth, but don't want to overdo it. I can see a soft green dress with spaghetti straps and a matching jacket; next is a black dress that looks dressy; it's sleeveless I have a small pin that has a humming bird with some sparkle to it. This would look nice with this dress. There are some black heels I can wear. I think the decision will be the black dress, as I hold it up to my slender built body.

I'm lucky I'm built just like my mom. We are both slender but we we're kind of short in height, so we still have to watch our diet pretty close. My father is medium built and has a lot of muscles in his shoulders and arms. We feel very protected when Dad's around. He's the problem solver in our family. That's what I'm looking for in a man I want to spend the rest of my life with.

Looking down to the floor next to my bed, I can see my gown that has slipped to the floor. It's flopping about looking as if there's a small ghost in the house. Picking it up, I say. "What kind of creature could this be?" When all of a sudden the small furry face pops out to let me know it's none other than my Donut, two small blue eyes and two small pointed ears. I give a kiss to that small head, as the small kitten jumps to the floor.

We had a busy day at work today, I had a lot of papers to file and some reports to type out. The weather has become warmer and everyone's looking for spring-like temperatures. I have stopped by the tanning bed several times hoping to have a little tan for the dance and the ceremony. When I make it home, unlocking the door I can hear my cell phone ringing. Searching though my purse, and finally reaching it, I say, "Hello."

"Sophie, I will pick you up at seven o'clock tonight. The ceremony starts at eight thirty. Can you be ready?" Barth asks.

I quickly reply, "Yes, Barth, I will be ready. See you later."

As I take my heels off, I see a little grey fur ball swiftly breeze past my feet into the other room. I go into the kitchen to fix a glass of tea. All I know is I have to get off my feet for a while and relax from the tiring day. Putting my feet up on the stool and sitting on the couch, I reach for the remote to watch the five o'clock news. Most of the news talks about the recovery of Brunner and how he will return to the jail here, to face a trial for his conviction along with some others captured from the site of the cargo ship.

While I think about the horrible ordeal, I realize how lucky we all were to be found and to be alive. I know that God lead Barth and the other officers to our rescue. Our police department is the backbone of our community. We need to be thankful for their protection. They deserve all of our respect, and we need to teach our younger generation how important they are to us all.

After finishing my tea and listening to the news, I get up and walk to the bedroom, where I take the clothes I want to wear out and place them on the bed. Then I proceed to hop into the shower. Enjoying the warm water of the shower, I feel as if I never want to leave such relaxation. But I know that I need to hurry so I will be ready on time. I also am looking forward to spending the evening with Barth.

When my shower is finished, I quickly wrap in the large white towel hanging on the rack, hoping not to get too chilled after that nice warm shower. Standing in front of the mirror on the bathroom door, I gently unfold the towel. Looking at the image in the mirror, I wonder what Barth would think of my body. My breasts are firm and shaped pretty good; they are not enormous but are medium in size. My legs are small, and my stomach is flat mostly. I try to exercise every chance I get. I'm not tall and I do not have long beautiful legs. I know that I have special feelings for Barth, and I think he must be perfect in every way. I fantasize his body next to mine. All of a sudden, a small fury foot is reaching under the door, reminding me that there's a life on the other side. I open the door to let some of the heat out of the bathroom. It has become quite.....steamy.... in there.

My black dress is figure fitting and slightly low in the front, and the small hummingbird pin looks nice to the side. I decide to wear my black heels with straps, so my freshly painted red toe nails showed. I have a small clutch purse that matched the heels.

Barth is on time as usual. As the doorbell rings, I open the door, and there he stands. The fresh smell of a man's cologne is in the air. He's dressed in a dark grey suit, a white shirt, and red and grey tie. Under his suit jacket he always wears his gun and his badge. His thick dark brown hair is very neatly combed, and he's close shaved. In his hands he has roses. They are red with some baby breath mixed. "Is your mom still here?" He asks, confusing me a bit. Then with a chuckle, he adds, "I brought her some flowers." He knows very well my parents have left a while back. I realize this is his way of making a little joke.

I answer, "She has returned home but I can put them in a vase for her." Then he smiles and admits he really brought them for me. He then leans over to give me a little kiss on the head.

Barth doesn't come in. It's getting late and we have to leave. We take the elevator to the parking lot and walk to his car. His car is a black Camaro with SS on the side. I am not sure what the SS stands for. It looks like a brand new car. As I climb in, I notice the interior is nice and the seats very soft. I don't want him to think I'm stupid, so I don't ask what the SS means. Then it occurs to me, it must mean super sport. He says, "It drives fast and is pretty good on gas usage." We head on down the road.

As we walk into the building where the ceremony will take place, we continue down a long hallway to a large room. There are seats on both sides and seats in the front of the room. There also is a microphone in the front. Looking around I see a lot of the children that had been abducted sitting with their parents. I do not see Calah. I don't know why she and her family are not here. Maybe they are just running late.

Barth and I move into the seats in the front row since he will be getting an award. As I look up, I can see Monica. Her husband is there by her side. She introduces him to us. Her son looks so pleased to have his Mom and Dad beside him. I look over at him and he gives us a large smile.

The Mayor of New York City begins with a small speech. His speech starts with how proud he is of the police department, and the Federal Investigations of the child abduction. The police department leads the presentation of awards. As they call out each officer's name, we all are very proud of each of them. Finally they call out, "Barth Cummings, leading federal Investigator, who stayed on this case until the children were found, arresting the ring leader, and giving us leads for the rest of the criminals having to do with this case. We want to award him with a special honorary award."

Everyone stands and claps. I feel so proud to be sitting with him. Barth makes his way to the front of the room. He gives a brief acceptance speech. "I want to promise each and every parent out there, I will stay on this case until we catch all of the people responsible for these children abductions. Also I will make sure that we all are informed when there is a fugitive, that has served time and been released, in areas that we might live. I am proud to accept this award," he says as he shakes the Mayor's hand.

The next award is given to Monica for her bravery in helping with taking down Brunner, and helping us all. I know that I would not be alive if she had not helped me. The speaker tells the audience of how she put herself in danger to save the children, her child, and me.

After the awards are over, Barth and I go to the dinner and the dance that is being given for the police department. We arrive at a place called Copacabana Club. It's pretty nice; the tables have white tablecloths; in the center of each table is a candle glowing on top of a mirrored square. Each napkin is folded in the shape of a small fan. The napkins are burgundy in color. These colors put a rich feel in the air. The waiter quickly makes his way around the tables to fill each of our glasses with the wine of our choice. We have a lovely dinner. Barth has steak, stewed potatoes, a salad and a glass of red sweet wine. My dinner is lobster tail with a butter sauce, salad and red wine. A lot of Barth's friends from the police department sit with us at our table. One couple is Mike and Brenda, and Barth's brother Steven and his wife Stephanie. This is the first time I have met Barth's family. They were very nice, just like I knew they would be.

After the dinner, the music began. The music is a mix of old and new, with some requests played. The band played great they were a local group. They certainly brought the place to life. I thoroughly enjoyed their music. From the look on Barth's face I knew he agreed. They played Y.M.C.A. and we all danced. Some line dancing is next and a lot of the guys don't dance but the girls do. Stephanie's a good dancer. I just watch her moves. We are having a great time. As I look over at Barth, he's all smiles. I can see that he's having a great time also. A new song begins, Macho Macho man.

"Barth, let's show them how it is done," Steven says to his brother, as Barth and Steven hit the dance floor. The other officers follow as all of the wives and girlfriends applaud.

"Sophie, look at our guys. They are pretty good dancers. Let's go put these dollars in their pants," Stephanie says with a mischievous smile as she waves them in the air. Stephanie has dark brown hair that was short, it is cut very neat. Her smile's very becoming. She also has beautiful brown eyes. She's thin and tall. Steven's built like Barth with light brown hair. Barth and Steven both work out. Everyone can tell, as they watch them do their little dance. I'm sure that physical fitness is needed for the type of job they both do.

Stephanie and I run up to place the money in their pants. The other girls do the same thing. As we are starting to leave the floor to go back to our seats, the tempo to the music changes. The Lady In Red begins to play. I feel Barth's hand reach for mine, no words are exchanged, as I feel his arm around my waist pulling me closer to him. I feel like I will surely melt to the floor from the warmth of his strong muscles next to my body. His breath caresses the side of my neck, as his lips gently touch my neck. I feel that we are the only people in the entire room.

The rest of the evening we talked with his friends and Steven and Stephanie. We had a great time. With each look exchanged between the two of us, it feels like two laser lights meeting and creating an explosion. With every touch of his hand, my heart skips a beat and my lungs feel a shortage of air.

As we drive back to the apartment, we both know he will be spending the night. As we reach the front door, I scramble to get my key out, finally reaching the key, I open the door. I have never been with another man. I wanted to save myself for that special person, someone I know that I am in love with. I know that person is Barth Cummings. Quickly turning around facing him, I feel my feet leave the floor as we passionately kiss each other. "Barth, stay with me tonight," I say.

"Sophie, you mean a lot to me. I'm falling in love with you. I want the first time to be very special," Barth says.

I do not understand; all I can think about is making love with him. "Barth, I am in love with you too!'" I reply.

Barth then picks me up and carries me to the bedroom. I take my heels off as he unzips my dress. His shirt is off by this time and his skin is pressed against mine. As we lie across the bed, I gently push Donut to the floor with my foot. She had been sleeping on the bed. As we make love, it is very special to both of us.

"Sophie, will you marry me?" Barth asks.

We have known each other for a while, but I knew the first time I laid eyes on him, that we were meant to be together. "Barth, I want to marry you. Yes, yes!" I coo in response and squeeze him tightly to me.

Chapter Nine

For the next few weeks, we do everything together. We go to ball games, the movies, even skating one evening. Our jobs keep us busy during the days. Some days we eat at the apartment and just watch television together. Barth asks that we not tell anyone about our engagement until we pick out a ring. It's very hard not to tell Mom and Dad, but we want to visit them and break the news together to them. And Barth's father, brother and sister-in-law, we want to invite to dinner to tell them.

Today, I am at work, and as my phone rings, I figure it might be Mom. To my surprise, it's Mrs. Johnson. She says she is Calah's grandmother.

"Hello, how is my little sweetheart doing?" I ask.

"She's doing fine. I need to meet with you somewhere. I have something to discuss with you," she says.

"Okay, we could meet at the Roaster's International Coffees Shop on Main street at five o'clock today," I tell her.

"That will be great," she replies. "See you then."

So as she hangs the phone up, I sit here trying to imagine what she needs to discuss with me.

"Sophie, can you bring me the files on Dickerson verses Dickerson?" Mr. Finch asks over the intercom.

"Yes, Mr. Finch. I will be right there," I reply.

The day is long and busy. I can't wait to meet with Mrs. Johnson. I would like to see Calah again but did not know if she will be coming along also with her grandmother. It's four o'clock. I have a few more files to file and a few more calls to make before I can leave. Time passes swiftly and the next thing I know it's four thirty, and I know I need to be leaving so I will be on time for the meeting. I quickly grab my purse and run to the parking garage to get the car.

Going down the street, I can see the sign in front of the coffee shop, a large red and white sign reading "Roaster's International Coffees Shop." There's an empty spot right in the front of the shop. Today's my lucky day. Pulling into the spot, I can see an older lady sitting at a table through the large glass window. She looks familiar, but I have never seen Mrs. Johnson before. I wonder if this is her?

After entering the shop, I look around, seeing several other people. None of the other people look like what I imagined Mrs. Johnson might look like. Walking over to the table with a pleasant smile on my face, I say, "Hello, are you Mrs. Johnson?"

"Yes, and you must be Sophie Lawson," she says with a pleasant smile.

"Yes," I answer, offering my hand as I sit down across from her.

"Sophie, I am Calah's grandmother, but I also am Marsha Johnson's mother. Do you remember Marsha from college?" she asks.

"Oh, yes. I remember Marsha," I tell her then remembering the last name. I ask, "Are you saying that little Calah is Marsha's child?"

Mrs. Johnson nods her head. There's silence for a while. Then Mrs. Johnson says as tears fill her eyes, "Sophie, Marsha was visiting with a friend out of town. I was watching Calah. She had been playing outside when she was abducted. I was worried sick until she was found." She pauses and then in a quiet voice, adds, "During in this time, Marsha was killed in a car wreck.

"I was so happy that Calah was found and was okay." Mrs. Johnson continues, as she sobs into a Kleenex she is holding.

I do not know what to say. "I am so sorry about Marsha's death!" I say with a shocked look on my face.

"Sophie, I miss her very much. I also know, at my age, I cannot raise Calah. I have very poor health. Marsha told me that Calah's father was a one night stand. She did not date any more after that. I understand that you are seeing Barth Cummings now," she states, eyeballing me with a hard stare.

"Yes, Barth and I are engaged," I reply, as my heart begins to sink with the thought that Barth and Marsha may have a child together. I think back to the odd way Marsha had acted about him every time I mentioned his name.

Taking a deep breath, I gather up the courage to ask, "Is Barth Calah's father?"

"Yes, I am afraid so," Mrs. Johnson says. Tears flow down my face.

"Why...Why didn't he tell me? I just don't understand!" I speak aloud, both to Mrs. Johnson, but also to myself.

"Wait a minute, Sophie," Mrs. Johnson cautions. "Barth didn't tell you because he did not know. You see... Marsha never told him. She did not want him to stay with her out of pity. They were young, and neither one was ready at that time to be a family to a child.

"I need you to tell Barth that Calah is his child. I know that he is an adult and responsible person now," Mrs. Johnson says.

"I don't know how I will tell him, but I will find a way," I promise Mrs. Johnson as our meeting ends.

I just sit here as she leaves the coffee shop, all of the energy totally draining from my body. I'm wondering how I'm going to tell

Barth the news. I'm also trying to accept the feelings I'm having about the whole thing. Remembering how I felt about little Calah from the beginning, I finally garner the strength to stand and go to the car. First, I go to the counter and order a hot cup of coffee to go. I'm hoping that the coffee might warm my insides and help me figure out what to do.

I barely remember the trip back to the apartment as I park the car. After entering the apartment, I just sit there staring at the phone, trying to decide if I should call Mom and talk to her about the whole thing. She's a very good listener, and my best friend as well as my mother. I quickly pick the phone and begin to call her number. I can hear the phone ringing on the other end. "Hello, Sophie is that you?" I hear her voice ask.

"Yes, mom, it is me," I say.

"What's up? Are you okay?"

"Yes, Mom, I just need to talk to you about something." My voice sounds upset I am sure.

"Okay, what is the matter?" She ask with concern in her voice.

I begin to tell her everything, but I start with Barth asking me to marry him. "Do you love him?" she asks.

"Yes, I do love him. I knew that I loved him from the start."

"Then what is the problem? I am glad for the both of you," she says, her voice sounding happy.

"I just found that he has a child. The child's mother was killed in an auto accident. Barth is unaware of the child, and I have to tell him. Marsha, my roommate I had for a while at college, is the mother. She and Barth were together before college and conceived the child. They were only together one time."

"Sophie, does this change the way that you feel about Barth? Can you be a mother to a child that is not yours and Barth's child?

59

Can you love this child the same as your own children?" Mom asks all of the right questions.

"Mom, nothing changes the way I feel about Barth," I say. "When I look into that child's eyes, I know that I love her also."

"Then you know the answer. Follow your heart. Everything will be alright," Mom said.

"You're right, Mom, thank you. I love you," I reply.

"Call me if you need me. I love you too," she says in response.

"Bye, Mom. Thanks again," I say.

As the night goes on, I try to relax and watch television for a while but I'm restless. The phone is silent, no calls from Barth. He had mentioned that he might be busy tonight. It feels strange without him. I have grown accustomed to his face. Donut wants to be my company tonight as she lies on the back of the couch playing with my hair, as I sit and lean against the couch. I decide to try and phone Barth but he's not answering. I guess he's too busy to answer the phone.

I fall asleep on the couch, and am awakened by the alarm going off in the bedroom. I quickly jump up to take a shower and get ready for work. I need to be at work by nine o'clock this morning. I have several appointments I need to set up with clients for Mr. Finch. Making sure Donut has food in her bowl, I hurry out of the apartment to the car.

As I enter the office, I can see Mr. Finch on the phone. "That bastard, he is on the loose again!" screams Mr. Finch!

Frozen in my footsteps, feeling the blood run from my face, I ask, "What bastard...What bastard...Mr. Finch?" The words finally come out of me.

"Brunner. He recovered in that hospital and they sent him back here for the trial, and now he has escaped! Last night he got away from the guard, somehow!" Mr. Finch, yelled out.

I have to get Barth on the phone. I need to tell him about Parker Brunner if he did not already know. "Party is unavailable; leave a message," his voicemail says again.

"Please call me, Barth, when you get this message," I repeat over and over. But I still do not get an answer.

A couple of hours pass. I try to do my work but I just can't concentrate. Looking out the window, I see Mike walking up to the building. In a few minutes, he's in Mr. Finch's office. Mike's one of the officers that was at the ceremony, and a friend of Barth's. Mr. Finch calls me to his office. "Sophie, I need you to go to the hospital with me," Mike tells me. Then he reveals, "It's Barth. He has been shot, he and Steven, his brother. They got Brunner, but there were shots exchanged. Brunner was killed but not before Barth and Steven were shot. Stephanie is already at the hospital. She asked me to get you to the hospital!" Mike further explains.

"How bad is it? He's going to be okay, isn't he?" I ask, my eyes pleading for him to say 'yes'

"I just don't know yet," Mike says with concern.

I grab my purse and we leave in a hurry for the hospital. My stomach is so upset, I fear I might vomit all the way to the hospital. I sit in the seat next to Mike in his police car, thinking *Oh, my Lord, please do not let Barth or Steven die. We need each other, and he does not even know that he has a daughter. This child needs him... I need him....She has already lost her Mother, please take care of them both.*

As we enter the hospital, the information receptionist instructs us to go to the third floor to wait until surgery is over. We are told that both Barth and Steven are in surgery. Going to the waiting area, we find the family is already waiting there. There's Stephanie and the guys' father, Mr. Cummings. I have not met Mr. Cummings before. He was out of town at the time of the ceremony and could not make it back. Stephanie introduces the two of us. He gives me a hug. "Sophie, Barth is so happy that he found you." Mr. Cummings says. "He was hoping to find the right person to spend the rest of his life with," He continues. He then has to leave, before he breaks down and cries. I can see this coming on, so both Stephanie and I let him have his space. He's a strong person and used to being the leader. Sometimes that makes it very hard to let others see your emotions.

Mr. Cummings is an older man, very handsome. He reminds me of Sean Connery, the actor. He's over the police department. He has worked for the N.Y.P.D. for a long time. I go over to Stephanie to comfort her. "Sophie, I don't know what I will do if Steven doesn't make it. He's my life. Nothing means anything without him!" She cries.

"Stephanie, I feel the same way. I want to be strong for Barth, but feel sick that it all could end. I have to trust in God to help him," I say. Then we are silent for a while and we just give each other a big hug. Later, I decide to go to the chapel to say a prayer. I start to enter when I hear someone else in the chapel. "God, you took Mary, the boy's mother. Now you are going to take my boys from me? How much do you think I can stand?" I realize I'm hearing Mr. Cumming's voice. I do not want him to know I heard him or to see him crying, so I just walk back to the waiting area.

After a couple of hours, Steven is in the recovery room and we are informed that he will be okay. The bullet had gone into the stomach, and exited the other side without damaging any vital organs. Barth on the other hand, has been shot in the chest, hitting the side of the heart. The doctor informs us, "This has damaged the heart , but we will try to repair it as much as we can."

I am happy for Steven and Stephanie. But I feel nervous about Barth's condition. He's still in surgery. Barth's father waits in the waiting area while Stephanie goes to ICU with Steven. As I look over at him, I want to tell him about Calah, but I decide that this is not the right time. Barth needs to be the first to know that he has a daughter. I will keep this secret until I can tell Barth.

Three hours into the surgery, the nurse comes out, telling everybody, "Barth is holding his own. The heart has a lot of damage but he is young and in good health otherwise. We are doing everything that we can. The surgery will last a couple more hours." She leaves to go back to the operating room.

Mr. Cummings looks so tired. He sits here with his head in his hands. He isn't saying anything. "Could I get you a cup of coffee?" I ask.

"Thank you, Sophie, That sounds good," He replies.

I place the money in the machine and bring us both coffees. The television is on in the waiting area. I hear the report saying, "Two officers shot in the line of duty, one was F.B.I. agent. Parker Brunner, the suspect, was killed at the site. An investigation will be done." I quickly turn the channel. Neither Mr. Cummings nor myself need to hear this news right now.

I hear on the intercom a voice. "Code Blue in the recovery, code blue in recovery!" My heart jumps a beat. I am not sure Barth has made it to recovery yet. We have not been informed. Mr. Cummings looks up with concern. I know he's thinking the same thing I'm thinking. "We don't know if it is him, we don't know!" I say.

After a short while, we have not heard anything, so we thought it is not Barth that coded. My nerves are getting the best of me so I decide to go to the bathroom to be by myself for a while. When I enter the bathroom I just lost it. I fall to the floor, tears rolled down my face. I feel that I am going to vomit. "Why God, don't let Barth die. He is a good man. He is needed by every one! We love each other. Why did you let us meet, if you do not want us to have a life together?!" I hit my fist on the floor angrily. I feel anger toward God! The tears will not stop.

As I sat there on the floor, I tried to pull myself together. I look toward the trash can to throw away the tissue in my hand, filled with tears. Someone has dropped a rosary, a beautiful blue rosary. The light shining through it gets my attention. Picking up the rosary, I know that God is asking me to say a prayer for Barth. My anger turns to sorrow, as I plead. "Dear God, please forgive my anger. Barth needs you to help him in this fight. All of the children need him to protect them from the evil that is here on earth. I know that he is your helper."

I leave the bathroom and return to the waiting area with Barth's father. My phone begins to ring, I quickly answer it, hearing, "Sophie, this is Stephanie. Steven is going to be okay. He is talking and the doctor said he will be in the hospital for a few days but should recover okay. What about Barth?"

"Barth is still in surgery. We haven't heard for a while. I will let you know as soon as possible," I reply.

I can see the heart surgeon walking down the hallway. As he gets closer, he says, "Cummings family? Are you the Cummings family?"

Mr. Cummings and I both jump up, practically shouting, "Yes, that is us!"

"We had a hard time with Barth. His heart stopped and we had to code him in the recovery but he made it. He is now in recovery and stable. We should have him in the intensive unit in about two hours. He will be on the vent for a while. The repair to the heart was extensive, but time will tell if he will continue to recover. Are there any questions?" The doctor asks.

We cannot think of any questions at this time. All we feel is relief that he is alive. Everything seems like a bad dream or something. I think the doctor introduced his name as Dr. Aura. He has very dark shin, black hair, and a small mustache. He is of foreign decent.

"Thank you very much!" I reply.

We decide to go to ICU to wait for Barth, and we can see Steven also while we were there. When we walk in the room, Steven opens his eyes. He looks weak and very sleepy from the medications. Stephanie decides to step out for a while to get something to drink.

"Dad, is Barth going to be okay?" Steven very softly asks.

"He's in recovery, he's stable," Mr. Cummings replies. "Just rest. I will keep you informed, Steven." He continues.

Steven goes to sleep after a while, and we go out to the waiting area for the ICU unit. Stephanie returns and goes back in with Steven in case he might be awake. I continue to wait with Barth's Dad for Barth's return to the unit. Two and a half hours pass.

"Is the Cummings family here?" The head nurse says, as she enters the waiting area.

"Yes," I answer.

"We will be getting Barth Cummings in room six in a few minutes. If you want to visit, two visitors at a time, please," says the nurse.

"Thanks," Mr. Cummings says.

Washing our hands in the cleanser, we buzz the door to enter. There, behind a glassed front, with the number six above the door, you can see a motionless Barth attached to the vent machine. His chest rises and falls with every breath, created by the force of the machine. Holding an oxygen level of 90%, he remains asleep, due to the medication to keep him comfortable for the time.

All types of medications run freely through his veins, tubes are everywhere. All we can do is just be there for him, hold his hand and talk to him. I gently hold his hand with all the tubes attached. As I lean forward, I say trying not to cry, "Barth, I love you. It's Sophie, I am with you. I love you!"

Wiping the tears from his own eyes, Barth's dad kisses Barth's forehead, "Son, I love you too. We are all here with you. Hang tough," he says. He then leaves the room for a minute so he will not break down and cry in front of everyone in the room. The nurses are in the room adjusting the IV pumps that are going off.

For the hours that follow, I continue to stay at Barth's side. I do not want to leave him. I know I'm not going anywhere until I'm sure he's going to be okay. It will be a while before I can tell him about Calah. He needs to be strong enough to hear the news and for all of our plans to go forward but I feel that God is helping him to get stronger, and when the time is right, we will start our lives together with our new family. Who knows what life will offer us in the future .The thoughts flow as I lay my head on Barth's hand and patiently wait for him to wake up.

My eyes feel heavy as I sit with my head laying across Barth's bed, holding tightly to what used to be a very strong hand, but now is lifeless with intravenous medications running freely through its veins. As I hear a moaning sound, I quickly look up at Barth. The vent is doing its job as his chest still rises and falls with every breath. "Barth, darling, I am here. Hang in there. You are going to be alright!" I say. "I know that you are uncomfortable. I will call the nurse," I continue as I turn the call light on.

"Can I help you?" The voice asks.

"Yes, Barth Cummings, he is moaning. He seems to be having some discomfort. Can he have something for pain?"

"Yes, I will be right there," The voice answers.

Barth's father has entered the room. He can see the concerned look on my face. "Is something wrong?" He asks.

"He is trying to wake up, and he seemed restless so I called the nurse," I answer.

When the nurse enters the room, she gives Barth some medication in his I.V. "This will help him be more comfortable," she says.

"Sophie, why don't you take a break? I will sit with him for a while," Mr. Cummings offers.

"I hate to leave him," I reply.

"You need a break. I will call you if there is any change," he promises.

"Okay, I will take a little break," I answer. "But, how is Steven? Is Stephanie with him?"

"He is weak, but he is talking. Stephanie is with him. The news media, they are trying to talk with him. Stephanie is keeping them out of the room for now." Mr. Cummings raises his eyebrows as he speaks of the news media. "Sometimes I think they aren't really concerned about the person, just about the damn story! You know what I am talking about?"

I nod my head as I leave the room for a brief break. I take the elevator to the first floor. There is a small dining area. People are everywhere. Some are talking on their phones. Others are looking at magazines. One man looks like a street person; his clothes are dirty, and torn. He's just standing around. He doesn't have any food or a drink. I wonder if he is hungry. As our eyes meet, I feel that I have to ask, "Hello, can I buy you something to eat or drink?"

He looks at me and says, "If you can spare the money, I would appreciate it very much."

"What would you like?" I ask.

"Do they have root beer?" He asks.

"Yes, they do," I answer, as I proceed to get a drink for him. I honestly don't think anyone else even notices he's there, or even cares.

"Young lady, would you care if I sit with you at your table?" The man asks as I hand him the root beer.

"I do not care," I say as I reach for his hand and to introduce myself to him. "My name is Sophie Lawson. A friend of mine is here in the hospital."

"My, name is Albert Hicks. I used to be a minister at a Baptist church, believe it or not, but I had some bad luck, and started to drink. And everything fell apart after that." His face has many wrinkles, and a scruffy beard that is full of dirt. His fingers are very dirty also. I'm sure that he has not seen a bath for a while. As I sit there I can smell old whiskey, and sweat making its way to my nose. I'm trying hard not to let him know my true reaction to the stench.

"Mr. Hicks, do you have a family?" I ask as I look at this troubled person.

"Miss Sophie, I have a son. I have not seen him for a long time. And the wife passed away. I just didn't have anything left to live for"" He tells me as he lowers his face to the table.

"Where is your son? Do you know?" I ask.

"The last time I heard from him, he had to serve time for a connection in drugs."

"I am sorry," I reply. "Maybe things will change for you," I say as I finish my drink. "I will say a prayer for you, and will you say a prayer for my friend?" I ask as I explain I need to return to Barth's room.

"I haven't prayed for a long time, but I would be happy to pray for your friend. Thank you very much for the drink," he says, as he waves bye to me.

I think...all the way back to Barth's room, *I hope that Mr. Hicks finds some peace in his life.* He seemed to be a nice person that just needs some help.

Anxious to get back in the room with Barth, I quickly wash my hands with the sanitizer just outside of the glass front room, where I can see Mr. Cummings standing over his son in the bed. I

Notice just how much they look alike, both are very handsome, with very similar characteristics. "How is he doing? Any changes since I left?" I ask, entering the room.

"The nurse said that maybe tomorrow they would take him off the vent. She said they have been reducing the work of the vent and he has been breathing on his own."

"I think that he is going to make it," I say as tears ran down my face.

"Sophie, I am glad he has you," Mr. Cummings says, as he leans over and hugs me. We just stand there for a while, as we both feel relieved.

We stay through the night with Barth, taking turns to be by his side, going to the waiting area every now and then to get a little sleep. I cannot wait for the vent to be discontinued. Barth has opened his eyes a couple of times, but cannot speak because of the vent. He also is very sleepy because of all of the medications. I'm hoping that once the vent is taken out, and the medications lowered that he can communicate with us.

The waiting room has several members from different families all around. Curled in fetal positions on the small couches, we have pillows and covers the staff has supplied us. We take turns trying to catch a few minutes of sleep, while our loved ones recover in the Intensive Care Unit. Sunlight peers through the windows as a new day begins. I quickly fold the cover and put the pillow on the window ledge, as I go back to see Barth and relieve his dad for a while.

Mr. Cummings sits in a chair next to the bed. His head bent over sleeping, he looks comfortable but I know he could rest a little better in the waiting area. I gently tap him on the shoulder, asking, "Mr. Cummings, I am back. Wouldn't you feel better out in the waiting room?"

"Sophie, Barth has been responding. He touched my hand and looked at me," he tells me. "I am okay for now. I will go out there in a little while."

I walk over to the side of the bed. Barth looks up at me. It looks like he tries to smile a little. I reach for his hand. I can feel him grip my hand. "Oh Barth, I love you. I know you are better. God has helped you through this," I tell him, as I lean over and kiss him on the cheek. I can see he is trying to ask something. I think it is about Steven. "Steven is going to be okay. He was shot in the stomach but it did not damage anything inside. The bullet exited. He is recovering."

The nurse comes into the room and says, "Barth's doctor wants to remove the vent. He will be in shortly. If you all would like to step out for a short while, we will let you know as soon as we are finished. Then you can return."

"Will there be any problems when it is removed?" I ask.

"There should be no problems. Barth has been breathing okay on his own for a while," she tells me.

As we leave the room, Mr. Cummings looks at me and says, "Sophie, please call me John. Everyone calls me John. I looked back at him and smiled.

"Okay, I will call you John from now on."

"I know I am old, but Mr. Cummings makes me feel even older," he says with a big grin.

"Why don't we go down to the cafeteria and have some lunch? I will buy lunch," John says.

We walk toward the elevator. "That sounds good," I say.

While we are waiting for the elevator, we hear the intercom yell: "Code Blue! Code Blue to I.C.U. We both turn from the elevators doors and hurry back to the seats in the waiting area. Our hearts seem to skip a beat as we wait for someone to call us back to

Barth's room. We know that we are not going anywhere until we know what's going on.

In about ten minutes, or so, a doctor comes out and takes a family into another room. You can hear the family crying. I feel guilty, because I'm relieved it's not Barth. I'm very sorry for their loss, but cannot imagine the pain I would feel if that had been my Barth.

"The Cummings family, please," a nurse calls out as she steps into the room.

"Yes, that is us," I answer.

"You all can go back into the room now," she says.

Looking through the glass, I can see that Barth's bed is in a sitting position. He's motioning for us to come in.

"Hello, how do you feel?" I ask as I get closer.

He says in a whisper, "Sophie, I love you. I wasn't sure I would see you again. Steven took the first bullet. He jumped in front of me. You did say he was alright; didn't you?"

"Yes, Barth, Steven is doing great. He may get to go home in a couple of days."

Barth's voice has not returned from the vent being down his throat. John walks up to the bed. "Dad, we made it through it all and I shot that rotten bastard. Tell me he died. He has hurt so many people, he deserved everything he got!" Barth says to his father.

"Son, it is over for Parker Brunner. He cannot hurt another family. You and Steven just need to get well. I know there are plenty of other bad guys that need what they deserve also."

"I know that some of your buddies at N.Y.P.D. can handle them until you and Steven are well again," I quickly add to the conversation.

We stay by his bed, feeling enormous relief and thanks to God that Barth is going to recover. Even though he will have to go to physical therapy for a while to get back all of his strength.

Chapter Ten

For the next few weeks, I am at the hospital each and every day after work. Barth's dad had to go back to work, but he came by after work also. Steven was released to go home. Stephanie and Steven come to the hospital often. They release Steven to go back to work after about a month.

I want to get Barth home before telling him that he had a daughter, the time needs to be just right. Physical therapy is tiring for him and often he gets out of breath, and becomes impatient. One day they had him walking on the tread mill. I came by and he was frustrated because he could not stay on it longer than forty minutes at a time. "I am going to run on this son of bitch for an hour, you watch me!" He yelled at the nurse, as I walked in the door.

"Barth, a little at a time, until you are stronger. You'll get there. You'll see, trust me," I encourage him.

"I'm sorry, I don't know what got into me," Barth explains to the nurse.

"Don't worry about it," answers the nurse. "Usually, we do not have people so eager to succeed. We have to coach them to continue the therapy." Then she smiled and patted him on the shoulder.

"Sorry, Sophie, you had to see me at my worst," Barth says as he reached for my hand.

"Everyone has a breaking point. I would not love you so much if I thought you were perfect," I assure him. "Here, I brought you a lemonade as I passed the cafeteria," I tell him with a smile.

Barth sits in his wheelchair. His physical therapy is finished for the day. I take him up on the elevator back to his room. He has been moved from the I.C.U. to the third floor in a regular room.

"Sophie, Steven was by earlier today," he tells me. "He's going back to work, Monday. Can you believe that?" He asks.

"Yes I think it's great!" I reply. "You will be going back before too long, just hang in there," I say.

"Do you really think I will ever be well enough to return to investigations?" Barth asks with doubt in his voice.

"Barth, you are a fighter. You will beat this thing. I will help you!" I reply.

We are at the room and I lean over and kiss him passionately. We sit in silence for a while. Then we both speak at the same time, saying, "I love you."

I help him back into his bed, and continue to lie beside him. Holding tightly onto each other, we fall to sleep. We sleep for a couple of hours. When I wake up, I realize I need to be leaving. I need to get home so I can make it to work the next day. "Barth, Barth honey, I need to be leaving. I'll be back tomorrow, after work," I tell him.

He reaches over and kisses me. "I wish we never had to leave each other again," he says.

"Me too," I reply. "You will be home soon .We will be together forever." I kiss him bye.

As I am going out the door, Stephanie, and Steven walk up. "Hello, Sophie, how is the big bro doing today?" Steven asks with a smile.

"Eager to return to work, and impatient," I reply, hoping Steven will cheer him up.

"I have to be running, I have to work tomorrow. See you, honey, later," I say, looking back at Barth. He blows me a kiss. "See you Stephanie and Steven," I say, leaving the room.

"Better relax while you can, Barth. The work is piling up for your return," Steven teased, looking at Barth, as he enters the room.

"We know who really works around here, and it isn't you," Barth teased back to Steven. "All teasing aside, what are they saying about Parker Brunner's death?" Barth asked.

"They are investigating several leads on other things that he was involved in. One lead was on a couple of kids found in a landfill beat to death, they were from Kentucky. Someone identified Parker, when the local police had pulled him over, for speeding in Kentucky. He had a couple of young people in the old Chevy truck he was driving. They think he was selling drugs back then, and picked the kids up while driving through Kentucky. There was a fight between the boy and him and he killed the boy and the girl. His D.N.A. was found on both of the bodies; the girl had been raped and beat to death. These were some of his earlier crimes about three years back, I think," said Steven.

Letting all Steven had said sink in, Barth said, "You know Sophie's parents live in Garrett Kentucky. I wonder if she knew this couple. I bet she remembers the murders. I will ask her."

74

"There is more people left in the child abduction ring, than we busted, you know that, Barth. I hope we can round them all up, but I can't see it happening right away," Steven said.

"I realize that, but we got some of the sons of bitches off the street, and killed some of them along the way," Barth said as he takes a drink of water from the glass sitting in front of him, on his bedside tray.

Stephanie just sat there while the two brothers talked about their work. Eventually, there was a break in their conversation, giving her a chance to say something. "Is everything going alright with Sophie?"

"Yes, she never complains of anything. She is a sweetheart," Barth answered.

"Have you two set a wedding date yet?" Stephanie asked, smiling from ear to ear.

"Steph, now how do you know we are planning a wedding?" Barth asked and smiled back at her. Then Barth has a very surprised look. "Oh, damn it, Steven. The ring is in the squad car. You know the one you were driving the night we got Parker. It's in the glove compartment," he told him, as his memory seemed to just kick in all of a sudden. "The ring is beautiful, two karats, a solitaire. I knew she would love it. She had been looking at one similar in a book," Barth said.

"Don't go nuts, man. I will check out the car. I have to go by the department tonight anyway," Steven said, frantically.

About that time the phone rang. Barth picked up the phone. "Hello, Barth Cummings."

"Hello, honey, just checking on you. I made it home okay," I say.

Out of the Dark Into the Sun

"Glad to hear your voice. I was getting very lonely without you," Barth answers as he looked over at Steven and Stephanie. They had already gotten out of their seats, and started toward the door. They just gave Barth a little wave and disappeared into the hallway, letting Barth know that they were leaving until another time.

"If I was there with you, we could make love all the night," I hear Barth lovingly say.

"I will close my eyes and pretend that we are making love," I answer. "I will see you in my dreams. I love you, Barth Cummings, forever."

"I love you, Sophie Lawson forever and ever," Barth answers.

"Goodnight, I will see you tomorrow," I say.

As I hang the phone up, Donut runs across the couch and jumps up to the back. She puts her front paws into my hair, purring and working her small paws through my hair, as if to give me a much needed massage. This is one of her favorite things to do. I sit for a while relaxing, then I help her to the floor and toss her a ball of yarn to play with.

I think about the wedding plans, but decide that it will be best to keep everything on hold, until Barth is home and back to his self, then I will tell him about Calah. Then I realize that I have not spoken to her grandmother about Barth's hospitalization or getting shot. I'm sure that she has heard the news, but she has not phoned me either.

I need to go to bed, but I plan to call her tomorrow. "Come on Donut, it is time to go to bed," I call out, hoping that that little furry buddy will come to the bed. I put on my pajamas and turn the covers back. I climb into the bed, and before I have time to turn the light out, I feel a small thump. Donut has jumped to the bed from the floor for her night of sleep. I then reach over and turn the lamp off.

Donut is my companion, since Barth is not here. She is warm and cuddly, and helps to relieve the lonely feeling that seems to appear at night time. I switch the lamp back on for a while, to set the alarm and decide to watch television for a while. I am fighting off the heaviness. My eyelids close and, then I feel myself fall to a deep sleep.

Chapter Eleven

"Waking up to your favorite Station! Playing Staying Alive, by the Bee Gees!" The alarm screams at me as I quickly turn it off. Feeling the cool air in the room, I pull the cover over my head, trapping the warm air around my body. I'm dreading facing the new day. Regardless, I don't want to be late for work.

Jumping up from the bed and running to the kitchen, I start to make coffee. I pushed Donut to the floor when I got out of bed. I can hear her meows, as she makes her way around my legs several times. "Are you hungry, girl? Wait just a minute I'll get you some food." I can see her bowl from where I'm standing. It's empty. Reaching into the lower cabinet, I pull out a bag of cat food. She quickly runs over to her bowl, as I pour the food in the bowl. "Here you go, eat up." I say, as I give her a gentle rub on her back.

I go to the bathroom for a quick shower. Afterwards, I pick out a pair of brown dress pants and an almond color, lightweight sweater. I put on a little makeup and style my hair. I, next, decide to have a blueberry bagel, with my coffee. After finishing, I grab my keys, purse, and briefcase. I'm ready to leave. I feel that familiar little body making its way around my leg again. "I know you don't like it here all alone," I say, as I pick up Donut. I kiss her on her head. "I'll try to be back earlier," I promise, as I lower her to the floor. She then disappears into the other room, as if she's saying, "Okay, see you then!"

I hurry to the parking garage to get the car. Coming to my car, I unlock the door and pitch my purse, and my briefcase in the front seat. Sliding into the seat, and locking the seatbelt, I then place the keys into the ignition. As the car starts, I look into the rearview mirror. Feeling the way is clear, I proceed to back out of the space. I catch an image of someone in the mirror! My foot hits the break with a great force! "Oh Shit! Oh Shit!" I say, as I nearly hit a man.

I struggle with the seatbelt latch for a second, and unlatching it, I open the car door. Running around the car to the back, I can see an older man with a soiled coat, and dirty hair. He looks up at me. "Mr. Hicks, what are you doing down here in this parking garage? I almost hit you! Are you okay?" I ask.

"I am alright," he answers. "I came in here because it started to rain during the night. I guess I fell to sleep. Sorry, I walked behind your car," he says.

"That's alright. I'm just glad you weren't hurt. What are you going to do today?" I ask. "You must be hungry," I say. "Why don't you come up to my apartment? My little cat would like your company. I have some food in the refrigerator. You can just lock the door as you leave."

"I could not put you out, like that," he replies.

"Honestly, you will not be putting me out," I answer. "You need a place to rest. Please feel welcome," I reply.

"Well, if you are sure, I could use a shower, and a place to rest for a while," he says.

So taking my keys from the car and locking the door, I hurry to the elevator as I lead him to the apartment, and let him in.

By this time, I am running late, so I quickly hurry back to the car and drive to work. Traffic is busy today. It seems that everyone is running late. I only live about thirty minutes from work, and about forty minutes from the hospital. It's very convenient to live in town where everything is. I finally make it to work. I pull into the parking garage below the law firm. I take the elevator up to our floor. As the door opens Mr. Finch is there smiling, "Good morning, Sophie. Are we running late this morning?" he asks, knowing that I'm always there before he is.

"Yes, I could not get it all together this morning," I reply.

"It's okay, Sophie. We all have those days at times," he says as he pats me on the shoulder.

As I walk into my office, I can see a stack of papers that I need to file on the desk top. Over to one side are notes with phone calls that I needed to make before the day ends. My day is going to be busy from the start. Then I remember, I need to contact Mrs. Johnson also today.

After filing the papers, and making a few phone calls, it's about eleven o'clock. I can take a lunch break now. I take the elevator down to the first floor and decide to get a hotdog and a coke from the food cart set up in the front of our building. This food service sets up each day hoping that everyone will buy their lunch from them. As I step up to the window on the cart, I can hear the man's voice. "Can I help you?" He says.

"Yes, I will have a hotdog with relish and a little mustard, and a diet coke, please," I say.

"That will be four fifty," The deli man says, as I hand him a five dollar bill. He hands me my change as he gives me my food.

After finishing my lunch, I decide to step back inside the building and sit on the couch that is located in front of the elevators. There's less noise here and I can phone Mrs. Johnson. The phone rings a couple of times. "Hello, this is the Johnson residence" a voice says.

"Is this Mrs. Johnson?" I ask.

"Yes, it is," she replies.

"This is Sophie Lawson, Mrs. Johnson. Sorry I haven't phoned you about Calah," I say. "Have you been watching the news? Barth had to be hospitalized. He was shot, and had heart surgery."

"I did hear about it. I knew that you would phone us when you could," she answers. "I have been sick also and a neighbor has been helping me with Calah."

"Oh, I am so sorry. Are you okay, now?" I ask.

"I am stable for now, but I have been diagnosed with Pancreatic cancer. That is why I am eager to find a good home for Calah."

"Mrs. Johnson, I haven't told Barth that Calah is his daughter. I know that he will be happy that he has a child. I just need to have the right time to tell him. He is better now and I think that he will be coming home soon. He has been in the hospital about a month now, and has been going to physical therapy every day. I don't know when he will be able to go back to work, but when he comes home, I will tell him then about Calah. Please, you call me if you need me to help with her. If you want, I could bring her home with me. I will phone you again." I remind her of my phone number again also. "Goodbye, I will talk to you later," I say as I end the phone call.

"Good bye, talk to you later," she replies.

I hurried back up to the office, so I can get my work finished for the day. Everyone in the office is busy in their offices. Usually we would say hello to each other but for the most part we are all very busy. Some days there are only a couple of us in the office. There are days when different ones meet with clients, or have to go to court, leaving the office kind of empty.

I am eager to get to the end of the day, so I can go back to the hospital to see Barth. Three o'clock has finally come and I am ready to leave. I grab my purse and briefcase and make my way to the elevator, waving bye as I pass Mr. Finch's desk. "See you tomorrow," I say with a smile. He's on the phone, but he manages a wave as I leave the office.

I make it to the car. Pulling out of the garage, I head for the hospital. The air feels good today. The wind is blowing slightly and the sun is shining brightly. I feel pretty good even if I am a little tired from work. While driving to the hospital, remembering that I left a house guest in my apartment today, I wonder if he has left and locked the door. And how he got along with Donut today?

I can see the sign for the Roosevelt Hospital and Trauma Center. As I continue to drive, I am eager to see how Barth is doing today. I pull into the parking garage and hurry to the elevator. I speak to each familiar staff member as I make my way to Barth's room. I can hear the television playing as I get closer. "Hello, honey how are you doing today?" I ask as I enter the room.

"Hi, sweetheart, I'm so glad to see you," he replies as he looks up from the book in his hand. "I really am bored until I see your face," Barth says with a big smile.

"Have you been out of your room today?" I ask, hoping that he will say yes.

"I have been out of the room. I went to therapy, and one of the guys from work stopped by. We went to the cafeteria for coffee, then he walked back to the room with me," Barth says.

"I think you are feeling a lot better. What does the doctor think?" I ask.

"I have good news!" He says, as he reaches for my hand. I am standing close to his bed by now.

"What? Barth, don't keep me guessing. Tell me, right now!" I beg.

He pulls me down to the bed and kisses me. "The doctor says that I can go home in a couple more days," he says. "But that is not everything."

"That is the best news ever. Thank God for everything. It is a true blessing. He has answered our prayers!" I say with tears filling my eyes. I am so excited that I don't hear that there is more to be surprised about.

"Sophie, I have had this for you. I just didn't get a chance to give it to you," he says as he pulls out this beautiful engagement ring, and places it on my finger. It fit just right.

"How did you know what size to get?" I ask.

"Well, I am guilty, if you are missing another ring. I borrowed it the last time we were together. I will return it as soon as I go back to my apartment."

"Barth, this is the ring that I loved from the book that I have," I remind him.

"I know you girls think us guys aren't listening, but we hear more than you think. I heard you say you liked the ring from the book." He kind of chuckled.

"I love you, Barth, I love you," I say as I kiss him.

"Sophie, you are the best thing that ever happened to me. Always remember that," he says, as he pulls me upon the bed beside of him.

I have asked Mr. Finch if I can take some time off to be with Barth when he is discharged from the hospital. I want him to move the rest of his things in my apartment. I know he will need help to regain his strength. We plan to set our wedding date, but need to take a little of time to get things straightened out. I have to find the right time to tell him about Calah.

Barth says, "The ring was in the car we were driving the night we got Parker, but Steven went to the department and got the ring and brought it to the hospital so I could give it to you, Sophie."

"He's always been your right hand man, hasn't he Barth?" I ask as I smile at him.

"He and Dad both mean a lot to me, you know," he reminds me, as he gives my hand a little squeeze.

I kiss him on the cheek. "Yes I do know," I agree.

We lay there for a while holding onto each other. The television is on but I don't think either of us really notice what is on. "Barth, has your dad been up lately to visit you?" I ask breaking the silence in the room.

"He came up for a little while this morning, but he is really busy at the department. They are still tracking people involved in the child abduction ring," he explains. "I guess they will never get them all but if they can get the leaders it will help a lot," he says. "We also confiscated a load of heroin and other drugs on the boat, the night we rescued you and the children. I'm sure that hurt their operation," Barth continued to explain.

I just give a sigh of relief... it is good to know that they are getting most of the ones involved. I do not know about the drugs, that the N.Y.P.D. and F.B.I. have confiscated, until now. Parker Brunner is one of the leaders. Thank goodness he is gone. He was an evil man.

"Sophie, they found out that Parker was connected to the death of a couple of young people from Kentucky," Barth tells me. "Do you remember hearing of this? The girl's name was Nicky, I can't remember her last name," Barth continues to say. "Anyway... they were both beat to death."

I pull my hand from Barth's hand. Sitting up from the bed, I feel the blood run from my face. I cannot say a word. I feel that I am going to pass out.

"Sophie, Sophie, honey, what is wrong with you?" Barth asks as he takes hold of my arm.

The tears run freely down my face. "Barth! Nicky was my friend. She was with me the night she disappeared. When they found their bodies, they were in a bag in the landfill! That scum. He raped her, and beat them both to death! I wished I had killed him!" I continue as I hit the chair next to Barth's bed with my fist.

"Sophie, I am so sorry. I didn't know that she was your friend, and you were close to her," he says as he gets up from the bed and holds onto me.

"It's okay, Barth. I knew what happened to them, but I did not know that Parker was the rotten person that did it to them," I explain, wiping the tears from my eyes.

I stay for a while longer to talk with Barth, but then decide to go home for the evening and check out the apartment. I had left Mr. Hicks there, and am hoping that he remembered to lock up when he left. I am hoping that he did not let Donut run out the door.

When I make it to the car, going home all I can think about is Nicky and Rick what a terrible death they both must have had. Parker never showed any signs of remorse, any way shape or form. He was so evil. What makes a person be so evil that he has no feelings for anyone else, not even an innocent child?

My thoughts go back to the day of the funeral. Nicky's parents could not stand having a closed casket, since this would be the last time that they would see their daughter. She was buried in her graduation gown, and her hat. You could see bruises on both of her hands, and around her neck. This indicated she fought back, and he had strangled her. Across her forehead was a large bruised area also.

This will forever be in my memory. She would have been so happy that her parents got back together. My thoughts fade a little as I pull into the parking garage at the apartment building, knowing that I am home, and Donut will cheer me up, with her playfulness.

As I come to the front door, I reach for the doorknob. The door is locked so I remove the keys from my purse. I unlock the door and step into the apartment. I can see that Mr. Hicks has left some lights on; that is alright I always hate walking into a dark room anyway but am trying to keep the electric bill to a minimum amount.

I don't see Donut. "Spooky, little cat, where are you?" I yell so she will know that I am there. Then I hear a little "Meow, Meow." Donut's sounds are coming from the bedroom. Tossing my purse to the couch, I walk into the bedroom. The window curtains are moving about. Donut is up in the curtains playing with the material. "I see you, Donut. Mommy is here, girl," I say as I touch the curtain, and she runs out. I reach down and pick her up, and give her a little hug. About that time the phone by the bed starts to ring. I quickly put Donut to the floor and pick the phone up, saying, "Hello."

"Sophie, this is mom. I was just checking on everyone. How is Barth doing?" Mom asks.

"Well we got good news today," I answer. "The doctor says Barth can come home in a couple of days. He is so excited. He just can't wait."

"That's great news, Sophie," Mom says. "Will he be coming to stay with you? I know that he will need some help for a while."

"Yes, he will be moving in, and after he is better, we will plan the wedding," I eagerly say.

"Wedding? Does that mean Barth officially proposed?" Mom asks, excitement in her voice.

"Yes, Mom. He gave me an engagement ring this evening when I visited him at the hospital. I can't wait for you to see it. It's one I looked at in a magazine and liked. It's so pretty."

"You know I can't wait to help with the wedding, but I realize we can't rush. Barth needs time to recover. You have each other. That is what counts right now," Mom says. She is always the most understanding person I know. "Well I am going to let you go, honey. Your dad will be home shortly. He stopped by the store on his way home tonight," Mom tells me. "I can't wait to share the news about your engagement with him. He'll be so happy too."

"Mom, before you go, I wanted to tell you... I haven't told Barth about Calah being his child. With everything that has happened, I was afraid it would be something else for him to worry about. I wasn't sure just how he would handle such news," I say, waiting for her wisdom to help me decide just how and when to break this news to Barth.

"Sophie, I am sure if he is the loving person you say he is, this lovely little child will be welcomed with opened arms. Don't worry. Once you have him at home, and you are alone, the right time will come and then you can tell him the news," Mom says.

"Alright, thanks. I will let you go. I love you and dad. Bye, see you later," I say, as I remind her to tell dad how much I love him. I could not bear to speak of Parker Brunner, or Nicky and Rick's death again. I decide not to tell Mom that they were killed by that creep. I knew she would see it on the news.

Hanging up the phone, I decide to make a tuna sandwich and a bowl of vegetable soup for my dinner. I go into the kitchen, as my little roommate follows me, hoping that I will fill her food bowl also. Turning on the radio in the kitchen and adjusting the channel, the first song playing is The Lady In Red. Closing my eyes, I am thinking of the night that Barth and I danced to this. Afterwards was the first time that we made love; Barth asked me to marry that night also.

When the song ends, I am brought back to reality. "Meow, Meow." I think Donut is saying, "In case you don't know, someone else in the house is hungry besides you. Opening the cabinet door, I remove her food bag, as she runs to her bowl, anticipating a full tummy.

Donut and I both get our stomachs full then retire to the living room. There are a few movies on television tonight but none seem to sound interesting. It is ten o'clock, so Donut and I decide to go to bed to rest. I was busy today and feel tired. Tomorrow I need to go to the grocery store, to stock up a little, since Barth will be coming home soon. I'm not certain what he likes to eat. Maybe I can make him a cake. My Mom's best cake is a Humming Bird Cake. Everyone loves this cake when she makes it. Barth may be on a special diet now because of his heart. However, he has always been very healthy, until he got shot and it damaged his heart. They did repairs to the heart. Maybe with diet and exercise, he will return to the healthy state he has always had. These thoughts run through my head as I sit there on the couch.

Going to the bathroom, I take a warm shower and put on my gown. Donut and I go to the bedroom and jump into the bed. I reach for the switch on the lamp to turn the light out for the night. It isn't long until I know I'm falling to sleep. I look over at Donut. She is in a small curl, purring, purring......

Chapter Twelve

A few days passed. Today is Memorial Day. Everyone is off from work. You can see flags hanging from the buildings. A few celebrations are going on also in honor of our veterans. I'm sure Barth's father is going to some of the celebrations. He had served in the Vietnam War. He's a strong believer in recognizing our service men. Also, Barth is being released from the hospital today. I went to the grocery store a couple of days before to pick up a few groceries. I hurried around this morning to prepare for his return.

Steven, his brother, is going to pick him up and bring him to the apartment. My Hummingbird cake turned out pretty good. I made it hoping that Barth would like it as much as everyone seemed to, when Mom makes it at home. She had e-mailed the recipe to me the other day.

I can hear the door bell ringing. "Yes, who is it?" I call.

"Special delivery, special delivery, for Sophie Lawson!" The voice on the other side of the door states. The voice sounds familiar. As I open the door, I find Steven, smiling from ear to ear. And behind him are Barth and Stephanie. "Please come in. Best delivery I have ever had," I say as I smile back. Steven steps to the side to let Barth enter first. Wrapping my arms around Barth, I give him a big kiss. "I am so happy you are finally home," I say looking into his eyes.

"I am glad to be with you, I didn't think I would ever be here again," Barth says as he kisses me back.

I can see he's a little weak still. "Barth, sit on the recliner here next to the couch. Put your feet up," I say. "I know that the trip home was tiring for you," I remind him.

"Look, Steven, she's already telling me what to do," Barth says.

"Get used to it," Steven answers. "I have," he adds.

Stephanie reaches over and hits him on the shoulder. "You wouldn't know what to do if us girls didn't tell you, you know that," she adds.

"Stephanie, you and Steven have a seat. Would you like something to drink?" I ask.

"Honey, do you have any beer?" Barth asks.

"Yes, I just picked up a six pack," I reply. "Steven, would you and Stephanie like a beer?" I ask.

"Yes, we will have a beer," Steven replies.

So I go to the kitchen to get everyone a beer.

"Hi, little kitty, you must be Donut," I hear Stephanie say, as Donut replies, "meow, meow." "I have heard a lot about you," Stephanie continues. Donut loves the attention so she takes right up with Stephanie.

When I hand a beer to Stephanie, she takes hold of my hand. "Your ring is beautiful, so have you two decided on a date yet?" She asks.

"No, we have not decided on a date yet. But now that he's home we will have more time to make plans," I say.

"Bro, you know I want you to be my best man," Barth says.

"I always knew that I was the best man," Steven answers, teasing Barth.

"What's your favorite color, Sophie?" Stephanie asks.

"I have always loved purple," I reply. "So I think I would like the girls to wear purple," I say. "I thought an almond color would go good with the purple for heels and accessories, and a traditional black for the guy's tuxes. That is if Barth agrees," I say looking over at him.

"Sure, honey, I am not hard to please," Barth says, agreeing with whatever I wanted.

"What about a flower girl?" Stephanie asks.

"Calah will be our flower girl," I say, before remembering that I have not told Barth about her.

"Calah? Who is Calah?" Stephanie asks.

"She's a sweet little girl that was brought back from the abduction ring, when we brought Sophie back," Barth answers.

"Oh, that would be great to have her for your flower girl," Stephanie answers.

"Sophie, have you heard from her family?" Barth asks.

"Yes, her grandmother phoned me the other day. She said Calah was doing great! Does anyone want anything else to drink?" I ask quickly to change the subject.

I know that I need to tell Barth the truth, but I want to wait until we were alone. I'm not sure how he will react to the news. He was very interactive with Calah in the hospital in Cancun, and she seemed to like him a lot. The thoughts of Calah keep going over and over in my mind......

"Sophie, Sophie, are you okay? Stephanie asked where the bathroom was at? You just sat there and didn't answer her," Barth says.

"Oh, I am sorry. I guess I was just thinking about us, Barth. I'm so happy you are out of the hospital," I reply.

"That's okay, Sophie. I know that we have all been through a lot in the last month. Besides, I'm a big girl. I can find the bathroom," Stephanie says.

"Barth, we need to be leaving when Stephanie gets back from the bathroom. If you all need anything, give us a call," Steven says.

So when Stephanie returns from the bathroom, they head for the door. Stephanie, and Steven give us a hug on the way out. "See, you later," they say as they walk out the door.

"Alone, at last!" Barth says. letting the feet down on the recliner. Standing up, he walks over to me. His arms wrap around me and pull me closer to his body. He begins to kiss my neck and unbutton the blouse I'm wearing.

"Barth, Barth, I have missed you so much," I whisper in his ear, as his kisses go farther and farther down my blouse. "Are you sure that we can do this? I don't want to hurt you," I tell him, hoping he will never stop.

"I will be alright. I can't go another minute without you, Sophie. Make love with me, I need you," he says. We manage to make it to the bedroom and undress.

My lips meet his again and again. I kiss his muscled chest and run my fingers slowly across the scar that is now healed where the bullet had entered his chest. "Barth, I love you. I love you forever," I tell him. Realizing how close we came to losing each other, we never want to let our lives miss every chance we have left to make love together again.

Chapter Thirteen

Sunlight, coming through the crack in the blind at the bedroom window, is evidence, we made love all night. Falling to sleep from sheer exhaustion, I hear, Barth say, "Sophie, are you awake? I love you. I have fixed us some breakfast."

I stretch, and yawn. "Barth, you shouldn't have. I am supposed to be waiting on you."

"It's alright, I am okay. I can do some things," he tells me. "I only fixed waffles and strawberries and some coffee."

"That sounds terrific!" I say as I scramble for something to put on. My robe is hanging on the bathroom door.

We both go to the kitchen. Barth has boxer shorts on and no shirt. He's such a nice looking man. He has muscles in his shoulders and arms; his hair is dark brown and cut very neat. He has a shadow of a beard, a flat stomach and a firm little butt. I am in love with everything about him. I know that we are meant to be together.

"Sit down, madam, I will serve you breakfast," he offers.

"Thank you, Barth," I say, and he reaches for my hand to kiss. After pouring my coffee and his own, he sits down at the table, across from me. "Barth, I have something I need to talk to you about," I say.

"Is it something bad?" he asks.

"No, but it might be surprising though," I tell him. "Do you remember Marsha? She was my roommate at college when I first met you."

"Yes, I think I remember her. I met her once at a party right after high school. We were to start college and some of us were invited to a party before we began college. She said she had just moved to New York to attend law school," he explains. "We all had a drink or two that night."

"Did you have sex with her?" I ask.

"Sophie, we were drinking, and she wanted to have sex. I know that we shouldn't have did it... but well... it just happened," he admits. "I have dreaded it for a long time. We never went out or anything afterwards." With remorseful eyes he asks, "You're not going to hold that against me or you?"

"No, Barth, you don't understand. Marsha was killed in a car wreck, a few years back, while she was out of town," I explain. "She left a child, Calah... she...Calah is your daughter."

"Calah is *my* daughter?" He asks with a shocked expression. "How do you know?"

"You see, Mrs. Johnson, Marsha's mother and Calah's grandmother, told me. Marsha told her you are the father. I hope that we can care for her," I tell him. "She needs us. Mrs. Johnson is dying with pancreatic cancer."

Sitting in silence for a while, I can tell Barth is trying to find words to fill the silence. "She's a beautiful little girl. I felt connected to her right from the start," Barth confesses. "I would like to have our D.N.A. matched, after all Marsha and I only had sex once. I hate to say, but the rumor was that she slept around a lot. I would like to take care of the little girl, with her grandmother being in such bad health," Barth says. "Sophie, how do you feel about this whole thing?"

"Barth, Calah felt very close to me also. You remember how she would not leave my side in Cancun? I wanted to protect her then, and I still do," I tell him. "I would like to bring her here to meet you and me together. When you feel up to it," I add. "I have not told anyone, except mom, I needed someone to help me make decisions. I didn't know how to tell you. But I knew it had to be soon. With Mrs. Johnson's health worsening."

"Sophie, I am ready for a family. Let's have her over as soon as possible. I know that you will be a great mother. Dad has always wanted a grandchild. I can't believe I did something before Steven," Barth says with a smile.

I can't believe Barth is so excited to be a father, getting married, and everything. This means giving up his freedom of being single, but he seems eager to change his life, and start on a new life with a family.

We both kind of forgot about the strawberries and waffles, and just sip our coffee as we sit there thinking about the changes we are about to experience. We spend the day together talking about Calah, and trying to think of things we all can do together.

I decide to phone Mrs. Johnson, and see if we can pick up Calah tomorrow and keep her overnight if she wants to stay. The phone rings a couple of times. "Hello, Johnson's residence," someone finally answers.

"Yes, Mrs. Johnson, this is Sophie Lawson," I say. "How are you doing?"

"I'm holding my own, except for a few episodes of nausea after chemo treatments. I am losing my hair," she continues telling me. "Calah has noticed that my hair is disappearing. I just told her I wanted to see how I would look without any hair. She seemed to be okay with that explanation."

"Mrs. Johnson, I told Barth about Calah. He was glad about Calah being his child," I tell her.

"How is he doing after the shooting?" She asks.

"He's still recovering. Each day he's stronger," I inform her. "I was wondering if we could come by and pick up Calah? Maybe tomorrow, if it is alright. If she is okay with it, we could take her to the zoo, and keep her overnight," I propose. "I think that we could ease into her living with us. After she gets used to us," I say. "How do you feel about this?" I ask.

"Are you sure Barth is up to having a child around this soon after his hospital stay?" She asks.

"Barth is doing alright. He is supposed to walk for exercise, and he is excited to see Calah again," I assure her.

"I feel she will be fine with it. She's an outgoing child. She talks about you all of the time," Mrs. Johnson says. "She can't wait to see your little cat. She said you promised her she could see Donut, your kitten," she reminded me.

"Yes, I did promise her that." I had forgotten. "I'm surprised that Calah didn't forget," I say.

"Calah, never forgets anything," she reminds me.

"Well, we will see you tomorrow, about ten o'clock in the morning. I will let you go for now. See you," I say.

"Goodbye, see you tomorrow then," she replies.

I hang the phone up. Calah is in kindergarden, but she is out of school tomorrow, and this will be the perfect time to go to the zoo.

"What did she say?" Barth asks, He's in the kitchen. I have phoned from the living room.

"She said it would be okay. We are to pick her up at ten o'clock tomorrow morning. Do you think you are up to going to the zoo tomorrow?" I ask.

"I feel okay. The walk will do me good," he answers.

Nine o'clock that night, we decide to watch a movie before going to bed. Barth wants to watch one of the "X Men" movies. I had purchased the movie just because I knew that was his favorite movie. I go to the kitchen to fix popcorn. I always like to have popcorn with a movie. "I'm making popcorn, Barth, do you like popcorn?" I yell from the kitchen to the living room where he's sitting waiting for the movie to start.

"I love popcorn. I haven't had any for a while. Sounds great!" He yells back.

After finishing popping the kernels, I bring a large bowl to the living room, for us to share. Sitting next to Barth on the coach, Indian style, my comfortable way to sit, I lean over and kiss him on the cheek. I sit the large bowl of popcorn between us.

"How do you think Calah will react to me being her dad?" Barth asks.

"She's young. She will be okay with it, I think," I reply. "Maybe, we have to let her know us for a while before we tell her that you are her father," I suggest.

"I think you're right. She has been through a lot, with her mother getting killed and her grandmother being so sick," he says. "My poor child. I could have been part of her life from the beginning, had I known about her. What was Marsha thinking about not even telling me about the child?"

"Barth, don't beat yourself up. She didn't want you to think you had to marry her just because she was having your baby," I tell him. "At least she didn't have an abortion. Thank goodness for that," I add.

We continue to watch the movie, until it's finished, but neither of us are really into it. All we can think about is Calah, and tomorrow. So we decide to go to bed. We both are restless as we lie there thinking about this sweet little girl, and how we are going to add her to our lives, hoping that we can bring some happiness to her life finally.

Chapter Fourteen

The night is long, but finally the daylight makes its way through the window.

"Barth, Barth, we need to get up it is eight o'clock," I say.

"Okay, honey, you want to jump into the shower first?" Barth asks.

"Yes, I will go put some coffee on, and get into the shower," I reply.

While I'm making coffee, the phone begins to ring.

"Hello," I say as I pick up the phone.

"Sophie, this is Calah's grandmother," a voice says. "I need to have Chemo this morning at eleven o'clock, could you and Barth pick Calah up at the hospital? It will be at the same hospital Barth was in," she tells me. "I forgot that my chemo was scheduled for this morning."

"Yes, we can do that. We'll see you both about ten?" I tell her.

"Thanks. See you then," she says and ends the call.

I go back to the bedroom to get in the shower, and tell Barth about the phone call. "Honey, that was Mrs. Johnson. She wants us to pick Calah up at the hospital. She has chemo treatment today, but she had forgotten."

"About the same time as we were going to take Calah to the zoo?" He asks.

"Yes," I reply.

"That's good. We won't have to drive as far," he says. He had remembered that Calah was from the Queens area. This is a rougher part of New York and farther than the hospital to my apartment. "Does her grandmother still live at Queens?" He asks.

"Yes," I reply.

We rush to get ready, drink a quick cup of coffee, and make it to the parking garage. "Barth, do you want me to drive?" I ask. I thought he might not be up to driving yet. This would be the first time, since the accident.

"Since Calah will be in the car, why don't you drive today? I need to get back in the swing of things, before I feel comfortable to drive with a child in the car," he admits.

So I get in the driver's seat and off we go. As we enter the hospital, and find the information desk, I ask, "Ma'am, could you direct us to the department that gives chemo therapy?"

"Yes, it is on this floor. Just go down the hallway, turn left and you will see the sign, Chemotherapy. It is right there," the volunteer says.

"Thank you very much," I reply.

As we turn the corner, we can see Mrs. Johnson seating in the waiting area. Her grey hair has thinned, and she looks to be older than her sixty years. Her face is wrinkled with worry, no makeup. She probably didn't feel like putting makeup on. Her clothes are simple but clean. She's looking in our direction and waves at us as we get closer. Next to her is pretty little Calah. Her hair is shiny, clean and looks like gold. Small natural curls hang all about her head. She's wearing a cute little sundress, yellow and white. There's a small overnight bag sitting next to her, and in one arm is the stuffed animal from the hospital in Cancun. Looking up from the book she holds in the other hand, she jumps from the chair. "Sophie, Sophie!" She yells as she sees us.

"Hello, Calah, how are you doing?" I ask.

"Are we going to see big animals at the zoo?" She asks. "Just you and me and him?" She questions as she giggles and points to Barth.

"Yes, yes we are," I answer. "Just you, and me and him," I say, smiling at Barth.

"Do you remember him? His name is Barth," I tell her as I reach down and pick her up.

"Yes," she says as she hides her face into my chest, very shyly. Barth doesn't know what to say. He reaches over and rubs her gently on the back, wanting to hold onto her but trying not to frighten her. I can see big tears formed in his eyes.

"Calah, are you ready to go to the zoo with us?" I ask.

"Yes, let's go!" She shouts.

I look at Mrs. Johnson, telling her, "I guess we'll be leaving if that is alright."

"Do you have a ride back to your home?" Barth asks her.

"Yes, my neighbor brought Calah and me over. She had some tests to be ran today also. She's in the X-ray area now and will be back to pick me up later," she says. "Barth, I am sorry, we did not let you know until now about Calah. Marsha, she did not want you to know. I, on the other hand, always thought you had a right to know," she explains.

"It's alright. I understand why she did not want me to know now. Sophie explained it to me," Barth tells her. "We will see you tomorrow," he adds.

"Bye sweetheart, I love you," Calah's grandmother says to her as Calah runs over to hug her granny bye.

When we get back to the car, I remember that I had picked up a car seat for Calah and put it in the trunk of the car. "Barth, could you get the child seat out of the trunk?" I ask.

"Yes, I'll get it for you," he says.

Getting the seat out of the trunk, he places it in the back seat. Calah smiles, saying, "My special seat, in my special car."

Barth, smiles. "I think I will ride in the back with Calah," he says.

I'm pleased that he wants to sit back there with her. Looking in the rearview mirror, I can see them both, Calah holding tightly onto the stuffed animal from Cancun, and Barth reading her book of three bears to her all the way to the zoo.

We finally make it to the zoo. Barth purchases the tickets while I take Calah to the bathroom. As we come out of the bathroom, Barth asks, "Are we ready for an adventure?" and smiles at Calah and me.

"We're ready. What shall we do first?" I ask. "I think we should get some cotton candy!"

"I haven't had cotton candy since I was a child," he says. "Calah, do you want some cotton candy?"

"Yes, Yes!" She yells, smiling from ear to ear.

It isn't long until we all have blue sticky on our mouths. Before we wash off, I have to get a picture, so I take a picture of us. Our next stop is to see the giraffes; the long necks are standing tall above the pens allowing the giraffes to eat from the trees nearby. They walk with pride from place to place. Calah smiles and points to them. Next we saw the playful otters swim all about in their small ponds, from one side to the other. In that same area, there are seals just to the other side of the otters, in their own swimming area tossing a ball to one of the zoo keepers. Calah laughs and laughs. I'm not sure who is having the best time Calah or Barth.

"Let's go see the elephants!" Calah shouts.

"Okay, elephants next it is," I say in a raised, excited voice.

After seeing the elephants, we decide to ride the train around to a few other sites.

"Who wants to be the horn blower?" the train driver asks, as we are boarding the train. "Young lady, you want to blow the horn before we get started?" He asks, looking at Calah. "I will help you, sit here with me and we can blow the horn together," Barth says as he helps Calah to his side. I sit just behind them.

"On the count of three, pull the string and horn will blow," says the driver. "One, two, three," he shouts.

Calah and Barth pull the string together. "Toot! Toot! Toot!" "Everyone buckle up and off we go," the driver shouts. Calah is holding Barth's hand by now and feeling very safe with him.

It is a long day, and we are all exhausted, but we all have a great time. We are ready to be headed home when we reach the car. After buckling the child seat, we are on our way back to the apartment. Barth rides in the front seat with me going home. He keeps looking in the rearview mirror at Calah. By this time, she is very quiet. Her eyes are closed; she's sound to sleep.

"Sophie, she is beautiful. I am glad she's my daughter. She is *our* daughter," Barth says as he reaches for my hand. He's so compassionate, and loving, not like some people; he cares for others. I know why I love him so much. We already feel like a family. When we reach the apartment, Barth gets Calah from her car seat and carries her in. She remains asleep, so he lays her on the bed, and covers her up.

Donut wants to go into the bedroom also, but I close the door. Calah has not met her yet and I'm afraid she might be frightened if she wakes up and Donut is there.

"Meow, meow." I can see that donut is not too pleased that the door is closed. It's as if she's saying, "So, there's a new kid on the block?"

"Come on, silly little cat. She will see you in a little bit," I say as I pick her up and take her to the living room.

Barth and I get something to drink from the kitchen and go into the living room. "I think she had a good time today, don't you?" Barth asks.

"Oh, yes, I do think she had a good time," I answer.

"We probably should wait for a while until I tell her that I am her dad, until she has been with us a little longer," Barth says with a serious look on his face.

"We'll know when the time is right, honey," I say, trying to make him feel better. "I know that you can't wait to love and take care of her, but we have to give her the time she needs."

The phone rings. Afraid that it will wake Calah. I reach for it.

"Hello," I say.

The voice on the other end asks, "Is this Sophie?"

"Yes," I reply.

"Sophie, this is Vera Johnson's neighbor. We were at the hospital where Vera was having her chemotherapy. I sorry to say she had a stroke. She has fell into a coma. I found your phone number in her purse. Do you have little Calah? We are at Roosevelt Hospital," the lady says.

"Yes, we have Calah," I tell her. "She's safe and sound," I assure her.

"The hospital located her sister from out of town. This is the only relative, they have found. She's on her way here," she also tells me. Then she asks, "Can you keep Calah, until they see if Vera will pull through this?"

"Yes, Yes, don't worry!" I answer quickly. "Thank you for calling us. Please call us again and keep us informed," I say.

"I will," she answers.

"Goodbye," I say.

"Goodbye," she answers. And we hang the phone up.

"Who was that, honey?" Barth asks.

My face has to be very pale, as I look at him. I just sit there for a second in shock. The words will not come out.

"Is something wrong?" Barth asks.

"Barth...Mrs. Johnson...she is in a coma ... she had a stroke at the hospital. They are not sure she will make it. What are we going to tell Calah, when she wakes up?" I ask.

Then we both just sit there looking at each other in shock. Finally, Barth says, "We can't tell her, not now, until we see if Mrs. Johnson is going to make it. We can't let her see her granny like that. She's too young to understand, not now!" Barth says, trying to protect the little girl from any more pain.

"I agree, Barth. We will help her through this," I say.

"Granny! Granny!" we hear coming from the bedroom, Calah is waking up and she's upset. She cries out again, "Granny! Granny! Where are you?"

"Sweetheart, I'm here," I say as I jump to my feet and run into the bedroom, throwing my arms around Calah. Barth is right behind me. We both are holding onto her. "It's alright, sweetheart. Don't be afraid."

"Where is Granny?" Calah asks.

"Remember you're staying with us for a while. We visited the zoo and saw all the animals," I remind her.

"I didn't see the kitty, Donut," she says.

I look down to the floor and there is Donut. Picking Donut up, I place her on the bed beside Calah. "Here is Donut, Calah. She's here, not at the zoo. She lives here," I say, showing her Donut.

Calah rubs Donut's back, Donut purrs and purrs. She's happy to have a new friend, and Calah is happy that Donut lives here and not at the zoo. "Can she be my kitty," Calah asks.

"Yes, she is all of our kitty," I answer. "You play with the kitty, and I'll fix all of us something to eat," I say as Calah climbs down off the bed. Kitty, Calah, and Barth all go to the living room, while I fix something for us all to eat.

I decide to fix spaghetti and a salad. I have some garlic toast too. This sounds good. "Calah, would you like spaghetti for dinner?" I ask as I walk back into the living room.

"I love setti. I love setti," Calah squeals with excitement.

"Then spaghetti it will be," I say with a smile as I look at Barth, who is sitting on the floor beside of Calah.

After dinner, we all retire to the living room to watch Little Mermaid on the television. Not our favorite movie but we think Calah might enjoy it. "Calah, what did you name your little stuffed bear?" I ask.

She held onto the small stuffed bear that she got in Cancun. Her grandmother had said she slept with it.

"Buttons. She is my Button bear," she replies with a big smile. "Granny helped me name my bear. Her eyes are made of buttons," Calah explains. The small bear is very soft, brown and has a small orange ribbon around its neck. The two eyes are two dark brown buttons.

"That's a perfect name. Your, granny is right," I say. As Barth picks up Buttons and tickles Calah in her tummy, she giggles as Barth and her roll around on the floor.

We sit there for a while, and the phone begins to ring. "Hello. This is Sophie Lawson," I answer.

"Ms. Lawson, this is Roosevelt Hospital. Your number was given to us as a contact for Vera Johnson, a patient here," a Voice says. "I am her nurse in the critical unit. I hate to inform you, but Mrs. Johnson passed away about fifteen minutes ago. She had been in a coma. That and the cancer was just more than she could handle. She had been through a lot, the last three months."

"Thank you for calling," I say. "I think she had a sister. Has she been notified?" I ask.

"Yes, she's here already. She was with her," The nurse informs me. "She's handling the arrangements. I will let you go. If there are any questions, call us back," The nurse says.

"Thank you, very much," I repeat as I hang the phone up.

"Barth could hear me talking on the phone. He doesn't ask any questions. He knows that we don't want to tell Calah right now. We will have to pick the time and the right way to tell the child of her Granny's passing. Barth has figured out what's going on from the answers given as I was talking on the phone.

The time is getting late. It's ten o'clock already, after Little Mermaid is over. I make Calah a bed on the couch. "You want to sleep with Buttons, and Donut, on the couch tonight, Calah?" I ask.

"Oh, yes," Calah answers as she jumps on the couch. She looks so cute lying there with the covers pulled up around her and the little bear. Donut is lying at the foot of the covers. It's like she knows that it's her new bed.

"I will leave the light on in the bathroom, if you need to go during the night," I say. "Barth and I will be in the bedroom if you need us," I remind her. But as I look down, I don't hear an answer. Calah's eyes are already closed. I'm sure she is tired from the busy day.

Barth and I walk down the hall to the bedroom. We both have a worried look on our faces. Thank goodness we picked up Calah when we did.

"How do we tell Calah about her granny," Barth asks, as we enter the bedroom.

"I don't know," I answer.

"And what about the funeral? We can't take her to the funeral. That is just too much for a five year old to understand!" Barth says angrily.

"I will figure it out, Barth," I say, as I turn the cover back on the bed.

"Come here, honey. I am just worried about Calah. She has had a lot of loss in her life. I want to protect the child, from so much pain. Hell, it is almost more than I can stand!" Barth says as he pulls me over close to him, and gives me a big hug.

"I feel the same way," I reply. "I will call tomorrow and find out what the funeral plans are. I think, that one of us should go to the funeral, and meet Mrs. Johnson's sister. We are going to have to tell her that you are Calah's father. We can keep Calah... forever as our child," I say. "I can stay here with Calah and talk to her about her grandmother," I offer.

"That sounds like a plan," Barth says as he climbs into the bed. We both decide to wear our pajamas tonight just in case we have to get up with Calah during the night. We are both very tired so it's not long until we both are sound asleep.

About three o'clock in the morning, I hear Calah crying out from the living room. "Granny! Granny! Where are you, Granny?"

I jump out of the bed, running into the living room. "Honey, it is alright! It is alright!" I say as I hug her. "Sophie is here with you," I say. "Why don't you and Buttons come into the bedroom with Barth and me?" I ask. She puts her arms tightly around my neck holding onto the little stuffed bear.

"Sophie, can we bring Donut?" She asks.

"I will take you to the bed, and come back for Donut," I explain.

"Okay," she says as she closes her eyes.

I place Calah and Buttons into the bed next to Barth and go back for Donut. As I pick up Donut, I hear "Meow, Meow!" It's like she is asking, "Can't a girl get any sleep around here?" I carry her to the bed and place her at the foot. "Purr, Purr...Meow" She kind of looks up at me for a moment, with the night light shining across the bed, in her spot. Sounds like, "Okay sister, which bed is it going to be?" I reach down and rub her head, and she goes back to sleep. Everyone is asleep; that is, everyone but me. I squeeze into the bed next to Calah. One leg is close to the edge. I can feel gravity trying to pull me to the floor. As I look over the peaceful faces next to me, a little girl finally with her father, I feel that I am meant to be part of their lives. The thought runs through my mind, *How am I going to explain to Calah about her grandmother?*

Chapter Fifteen

The morning came fast. "Good morning, honey, did you get any sleep last night?" Barth whispers, trying not to wake up Calah, who is all stretched out with Buttons and Donut on the bed.

"I couldn't sleep. All I thought about was how to tell Calah about her grandmother," I reply, whispering also. We go into the kitchen to make coffee, and to talk. "After we finish our coffee, I will phone the hospital to see if I can find out what funeral home the body was sent to," I tell him as I pour the water into the coffee pot. "Would you like some breakfast?" I ask.

"Just a bagel, and cream cheese, with our coffee, is good enough for me," Barth replies.

So I fix blueberry bagels and cream cheese with our coffee. When we finish, I pick up the phone to call the hospital. "Roosevelt Hospital," the information operator says.

"Could you connect me to the I.C.U. unit please?" I ask.

"Yes, one moment please," she says.

I can hear the phone ring on the next floor. "This is the I.C.U. unit," the nurse says. "Can I help you?"

"Yes, I am a contact person for Mrs. Vera Johnson, who passed away last night. I was trying to find the name of the funeral home that the body was sent to?" I tell her.

"Her sister took care of the arrangements," she replies, then adds, "Let me check for you. Just a moment please." Putting me on hold, after a few minutes, the nurse is back with the information. "Ma'am, Mrs. Johnson was taken to All Faiths Funerals, located at 189-06 Liberty Avenue, in Queens," she says as she continues to give me their phone number.

"Thank you," I reply as I hang the phone up.

I proceed to call the funeral home to find out the times she can be seen. They have informed me that the body will be seen tonight, and the services are in the morning at ten o'clock. "Sophie, I will go to the funeral tomorrow, and you can stay with Calah, and talk to her about her grandmother," Barth says as he pours himself another cup of coffee.

In about another thirty minutes, a small voice can be heard from the bedroom. Barth and I slip down the hallway to the bedroom, peeping into the doorway. There stands Calah holding her bear, talking to Donut. "Mr. Buttons, this is your new friend Donut. Can you say hi?" She asks her bear.

"Isn't that adorable?" I say to Barth, as we both stand smiling looking into the room.

Calah turns and sees us.

"Good morning, sweetheart," we both say.

Looking over at Donut, I can see that she isn't too happy to have a button-eyed, stuffed bear for a new friend. I give her another little rub on the head, and she continues to hold her position at the foot of the bed. As we leave the bedroom for the kitchen, I ask Calah, "Would you like some cereal and some orange juice for breakfast?"

"Yes, but I need to go potty first," she says.

So I take her to the bathroom. I had let Calah sleep in her shorts set. She didn't have night clothes in her bag. She only had another pair of panties and another shorts outfit for today. When we get to the kitchen for Calah to eat some breakfast, I say to Barth "I guess we need to go shopping for Calah some clothes today. She only has one more outfit for today. I guess things were so stressful and it was hard to think of everything, for Mrs. Johnson, considering her condition."

"Calah, do you want to go to the store and buy some new clothes today?" Barth asks.

"New clothes for me?" She yells.

When she finishes her breakfast, Barth chases her into the living room, as she giggles all the way. "Okay you two, go watch cartoons, until I clean the kitchen. Then it's bath time for us all," I say.

After cleaning the kitchen, I go gather some clean towels and washcloths for the bathroom. I run some warm water in the bathtub for Calah's bath. "Bath water is ready, Calah. Come in here and I will help you with your bath!"

"Okay, here I come," Calah answers.

She's there in a flash. I help her take off her clothes. "In you go," I say.

"Can Donut take a bath with me?" She asks.

Looking down at her bear she has dropped to the floor. I am at lost for words for a second. Looking out the bathroom door and over at Donut, on the bed, wide awake now, there seems to be a caption over the cat's head reading: "You have got to be kidding. Tell the kid we don't like water!"

"Well, Calah, cats don't like water. They hate it," I explain.

"What if they get dirty?" She asks.

"They lick their fur and feet to clean them," I try to explain, as I put soap on her back, arms, and legs.

"Can I do that the next time I get dirty?" Calah asks with a devilish smile.

"Calah, your tongue is not rough like a cat's so we are supposed to use a washcloth."

"Oh, Okay," she says contently. I am glad because I am running out of answers.

After everyone is bathed and dressed, we decide to go down the street to a children's clothing shop. We drive for a short distance before we can see the large sign reading: "The Little Tot's Clothing Shop." There are a couple of parking spots, just down the street from the shop. We pull over to the street side. We all get out of the car, lock it and put money in the meter.

"Calah, hold my hand. The street is very busy with cars."

"Okay," she says as she reaches for my hand.

"Sophie, you and Calah go on in the shop and look. I thought I saw Steven go into the building down the street. I want to check. See you in a moment. Okay?" Barth asks.

"Sure, we will be in the shop for a while," I answer.

Calah's eyes are all excited as we walk into the shop. There are several other people in the shop, one lady and a little girl with dark brown hair. She has her hair in French braids in the back. I remember when mom used to French braid my hair when I was small. I loved it that way. Another man is with his little boy. They have clothes for boys and girls.

"Sophie, can I have this?" Calah asks holding up a cute little sundress. It is blue with flowers on it.

"Let's see if they have your size." I figured she would take size five. "Here is a size five," I say. "We will get several things and go try them on. Okay, Calah?" I ask.

"I can have more than one?" She asks.

"Yes, I think we need to get several things," I reply.

We found several shorts outfits, some little panties, pajamas, and a gown with Disney characters, which Calah had picked out.

"Sophie, these are cute!" Calah says as she picks up a package with hair barrettes in it.

"I think we should get those also," I say, smiling at Calah.

We shop for a while, and pay for our purchases. I don't see Barth. He has been gone for a while. I'm beginning to worry about him.

"Where is Mr. Barth?" Calah asks.

"I am not sure," I answer. "But I'm sure he will be back soon."

Calah and I sit on a bench in front of the store, to wait for Barth's return. After about fifteen minutes, we can see Barth walking toward us.

"Sophie! There he is!" Calah shouts as she sees Barth coming down the sidewalk.

We both wave at him, smiling. "We bought a lot!" Calah yells out.

"So, you two bought the store out did you?" He asks, laughing at us.

"We did buy a lot of clothes for Calah," I answer. "They were all so cute. We will have to let her model for you, in her new clothes, when we get home," I say.

"So, are we ready to go back to the car?" Barth asks.

"I think that we are," I answer.

We walk to the car, unlock it, and climb into the seats.

"Did you find Steven?" I ask as he starts the car.

"No, and I don't understand. His squad car was parked about five spots from ours. The building was empty, where I thought that I saw him go into. The door was open, so I yelled for him, but I didn't hear him yell back," Barth continues to explain. "I tried to call him on his cell phone, but he didn't answer."

"Don't worry, Barth, just call him when you get home. He will be home then," I say.

Barth looks over his shoulder, pulls away from the curb, and enters into the traffic. Barth felt better today and felt that he needed to start driving again. I am glad. I really don't like to drive all that much. He's the better driver, anyway. He is very cautious.

"I need to go by the apartment to pick up clothes. All I have is jogging clothes, at your apartment, Sophie," Barth says.

"That's fine," I reply. Actually I have never seen Barth's apartment. I am looking forward to see the man cave. I know that Barth needed dress clothes to wear to the funeral.

Looking into the back seat, Calah sits in her car seat. She has already fallen to sleep.

"I guess the shopping wore Calah out. She is already, asleep," I say to Barth.

He turns to see Calah's little face, looking so peaceful. "She is beautiful. I can't wait for Dad, Steven, and Stephanie to see her," Barth says with a smile on his face.

We are turning onto Madison Street, where Barth's apartment is. His apartment is close to the Police Plaza. We next turn into the parking garage. Calah's beginning to move around in the back seat.

"Honey, are you waking up?" I ask. "We are here," I say. "Do you want to go up, and see Barth's apartment?"

"I thought he lived with you," she answers.

"He hasn't moved all his things yet. We need to pick a few things up here," I tell her.

I open the door, get out and open the back door. Unlatching the car seat, I help Calah to the floor. She very quickly runs over to hold onto Barth's hand, for the trip up to his apartment. I walk behind them to the elevator to take us to the third floor. Barth's eyes portray the love he already has for Calah, every time he looks down at her. As we enter the elevator, Calah asks, "Can I push the button?"

"Number three is the floor we are going to. Push three, Calah," Barth says.

So up we go to the third floor. When Barth opens the door, we see a large leather couch sitting in the living area, with a table lamp to either side. They are brass. There's a bar with bar stools. It's mahogany, with a mirror behind it. A couple of bottled wines sit on the bar. A small kitchen area is to the side, off from the living room. Two large doors open from the other side of the living room, leading to the bedroom. There is a king-size bed, that is unmade with a few dirty clothes about on top. There's a few scattered papers lying on the bedside tabletop.

"Sorry the place is such a mess," Barth apologizes.

"It's okay, Barth, it looks better than my apartment," I answer, looking around in amazement.

Calah runs to the bed to jump on it since it was so large. Barth puts his hands on the bed pushing downward with every jump, helping her go higher and higher! Calah shouts, "Look Sophie, Look!" As she giggles and giggles.

Barth gathers some of his clothes, including a black suit, white shirt, and a tie with a touch of red in it. He has two gym bags and some hanging clothes to take back to the car. "I think I will try to call Steven again. Please, if you want something to drink, there are some drinks in the refrigerator. Sophie, get you and Calah something," he says.

"Okay, Ms. Calah, what would you like to drink?" I ask. "How about a small can of orange juice?" I ask as I open the refrigerator door seeing the juice.

"Okay," Calah replies.

I decide to drink some bottled water, as I hear Barth on the phone. "Hey, bud, where have you been? Not answering your phone these days? I thought that I saw you today. I saw the squad car parked down by The Little Tots Clothing Store. Did you go into the vacant building down there?" Barth asks.

"No, man, it wasn't me," Steven answered. "Someone may have borrowed the car," He said. "Why were you down to a child's clothing store?" Steven asked Barth.

"We were just checking the store out for some of the children that Sophie knows." I hear Barth explain. He's not ready to tell him about Calah yet.

"How are you and Stephanie doing these days?" Barth asks.

"We're okay. It has been really busy at the station. You know how it is, Barth," Steven continued to explain.

"Has Dad been in town or out of town working these days?"

"He just returned to town last night. He was at the station today," Steven replied.

"Sophie and I want to have you guys over for dinner one night."

"Sure, sounds good, Bro," Steven said.

"I'll talk to you later," Barth says, ending the conversation.

"Okay, see you later," Steven replied.

We finish our drinks, and lock the apartment, and drive back to my apartment. Barth is quiet the whole way. He doesn't say anything about the phone call to Steven. He just has a puzzled look on his face. I feel he will talk about what's bothering him later. So I don't say anything either.

As we enter the apartment, Calah gets busy playing with Donut and Buttons. Barth and I just sit down for a moment. "Do you want to order pizza for dinner," I ask.

"That sounds great," Barth answers.

"Calah, do you like pizza?" I ask.

"Yes, Donut likes pizza too," Calah shouts back from the bedroom where she has followed Donut to play.

I pick up the phone and call the nearest pizza Shop. The phone rings once. "Hello, New York's Favorite Pizza. Our special is one large with three toppings, for Fourteen dollars, delivery free," the voice says.

"That sounds good. We would like pepperoni, sausage, extra cheese, and add black olives, please," I say.

"Alright, we will be there in thirty minutes. Your total will be fifteen dollars and thirty cents," the voice says again.

"Okay, thank you very much," I reply, and hang the phone up. "Barth, I could tell you seemed upset, after talking to Steven. Was something wrong?" I finally ask.

"I'm not for sure," Barth admits. "I know that he was lying to me. I just can't figure why," Barth says. "I could always tell when he was lying. The sound of his voice changes. I have learned to recognize this," Barth explains.

"Maybe, he could not tell you then," I say.

"No, that's not it, Sophie. We work together. We tell each other everything," He says, sounding very upset.

"Barth, just let it go. You can ask him later," I say, trying to comfort him. But, I also am wondering what is really going on.

Calah comes running into the living room, all excited. Jumping into Barth's lap, she asks, "Can I be your model now? I want to see all my new clothes," she says, smiling at both of us, without a worry in the world. I thought it would be great if you could capture all this innocence, put it into a bottle and take a dose when you felt most troubled about something.

"Yes, we are excited to see how beautiful you look in those new clothes," Barth tells her as she jumps down.

"I will help you change, Calah, in the bedroom," I say as we walk into the bedroom. "Barth, will you listen for the pizza delivery?" I yell.

"Okay!" Barth yells back.

Calah wants to try on the blue sundress first. She looks so cute. She runs to the living room to show Barth. "Here I am, Mr. Barth, do I look beautiful?" She asks as she turns around and around.

"Calah, you do look beautiful. You don't have to call me Mr. Barth," he tells her.

"What do you want me to call you?" She asks as she looked up into Barth's eyes.

I know that he cannot wait another minute to tell her that he is her father. Barth picks her up and sits her back on his lap. "Calah, I want to tell you something," he says.

"Will it be our secret? Can Sophie know?" She asks looking up at me.

"I will tell you both together," he says. He kisses her on the forehead. "You are the best thing that ever happened to me," he continues to say. "I want you to call me Dad," he says.

Calah looks a little puzzled. "I never saw my Dad," she says. "My mom said he went away," Calah reveals.

"Your mom, Marsha, and I met a long time ago. I never knew about you until now. Your Granny told me you were my little girl," he tells her. "I love you very much, and will always be your Dad, Calah," Barth says with tears in his eyes.

I reach down and hug them both.

"My mommy is in heaven," Calah says. "She had to go and help Jesus do something, Granny told me," Calah adds. "But we will see her again, someday, when she finds a house there."

"Maybe you can live with Sophie and me until then," Barth says. "And you can call me Dad."

"Okay," Calah says as she wipes the tears from Barth's cheek with her small finger.

The doorbell rings. The pizza delivery man is at the door. "Barth, do you have money for the pizza, or I could write a check," I tell him.

"Sophie, I have a twenty, just give him that. He can keep the change for his tip."

I open the door, saying, "Hello."

"Pizza delivery, ma'am, one large three toppings," the guy says.

"That is it, thank you," I say, handing him the money. "Just keep the change," I add, as I close the door.

We watch television that night, have pizza, watch Calah try on all of her new clothes, and then go to bed. It has been a busy day. The next morning, after breakfast, Barth starts getting ready to go to Mrs. Johnson's funeral. Calah and I are going to stay home and talk about things. Calah helps me put the dishes into the dishwasher.

"We do not have a dishwasher at my house," Calah says. "I have my special stool I stand on to help granny wash dishes."

"Calah when I was a little girl, like you, we didn't have a dishwasher either. I stood on a small stool to reach the sink also," I tell her. "When I was about twelve years old, my dad bought mom a dishwasher," I say.

Donut is in the kitchen, eating from her food bowl, listening to our conversation, happy Calah is occupied with something else for a while. "We could probably put Donut in the dishwasher for a bath," Calah says, as she giggles a little. Donut coughs up a fur ball, and quickly runs out of the kitchen. She wasn't taking any chances of getting a bath in the dishwasher.

"I think that the dishwasher would be too much for Donut. We probably should not do that," I remind Calah.

Barth walks into the kitchen, smelling so good. "Well, girls I will be back in a short while," he says as he gives us both a kiss. Calah, and I both are speechless.

"You are beautiful!" Calah finally says.

Barth has on the suit, white shirt, and tie. He's one good looking guy. "Thank you, Calah," he says.

"Watch, or all the girls will want to follow you home today," I say, picking at him.

"There's only one girl for me, you know who that is," he says, looking at me.

"It's me!" Calah says, putting her hands on her hips.

"I take that back. There are only *two* girls for me, Calah and Sophie," he says, smiling at the two of us.

"Okay, we will see you when you get back," I say as he walks out of the door. "Calah, let's go into the living room and color. I have some crayons and a coloring book here. I color sometimes just for fun, if I have nothing else to do," I say.

"Okay," she says.

The coloring book has a lot of kittens in it, and flowers. We go into the living room to put it on the coffee table. "There we go, we can color the kittens and make them so cute," I say lying the book down. "Calah, you know granny has been very sick," I say slowly.

"She is in the hospital. The doctor will heal her," Calah says.

"Sometimes the doctor can't fix what is wrong, so we have to go somewhere else to be fixed. You know how sometimes we break something...something we like very much but we can't fix it. We don't have that toy anymore but we get a new toy. We are happy about the new toy, but we never forget the old toy," I try to explain. "Granny is going to heaven so God will fix her. She will be with Marsha, your mommy. She will be happy to see her. She will get well, and never be sick again," I remind her.

"Can I see Granny again when she gets well?" Calah asks.

"Someday, you can see her again. Why don't we say a prayer to Granny? She will hear us from heaven," I say.

Calah folds her small hands, and closes her eyes. "Granny, say hello to Jesus for me. Tell him to make you better, and mommy better. Ask him to fix my room pretty in purple, for when I come and visit you and mommy. Don't forget to tell mommy, I found Daddy. I will be here with Sophie and him, until I can visit you. I'll be a good little girl. I love you and Granny. Amen. This is Calah," she says.

Then a moment later, she picks up another crayon and looks up at me, saying, "We could color this kitty grey just like Donut."

I thought to myself, *Calah understands what I told her and accepts it okay. There's no need to dwell on it any longer.* She is amazing for a child of her age. "Yes, Calah, that color will be great," I say and pick up another crayon.

Chapter Sixteen

For the next two weeks, we stay busy with Calah. We don't mention anything about Granny's funeral. School is out for the summer. I am hoping to get Calah in a school about fifteen miles from the apartment, next year. Also Barth and I have talked about finding a house. This would give us more room and Calah can have her own room.

Barth met Mrs. Johnson's sister at the funeral. He says she's tall and slender, with grey hair. She's about a year or so younger than Vera. She's very friendly. Vera had told her already about Barth being Calah's father. She's happy that he has accepted Calah with open arms as his child. She lives out of town, and is returning to her home, following the funeral. She gave us her phone number. She wants us to keep her informed about Calah.

The last visit to the doctor, for Barth, goes great. The doctor tells us Barth can return to work on the following Monday. I also have to return to work. Mr. Finch has been very understanding with me, allowing me to stay home to be with Barth and Calah, but things are looking up. So, we have to get back to a normal routine.

"Sophie, let's call Dad, Steven and Stephanie and invite them over for dinner tonight. I need to celebrate going back to work, and I want to tell them about Calah," Barth explains.

"That sounds great," I answer. "What shall I fix?"

"I could sit the grill out on the balcony. We could grill steaks out there," he says.

"Okay steaks, baked potatoes, salad, and strawberries for desert," I say.

"Strawberries!" Calah chimes in. "I love strawberries." She then pitches a ball across the floor, hoping that Donut will chase it. Donut doesn't show much interest in the ball, as she goes into the kitchen for a drink of water.

Barth picks the phone up to call his Dad. "Hello," His Dad said on the other end.

"Dad, Sophie and I want to have you guys over tonight, for dinner. Are you busy?" Barth asks.

"No, I am not busy tonight. As a matter of fact, I was thinking of phoning you, to see how you were doing. I haven't heard from you for a while," he says.

"I know I haven't called you for a while. We are doing great! I got the okay to return to work Monday, and we wanted to celebrate with you guys, Steven, Stephanie and you." Barth says.

"Have you talked to Steven yet?" His dad asks.

"No, I haven't called them yet," Barth replies.

"He has been a hard person to reach these days also," explained John, Barth's dad.

Barth tries several times to reach Steven and Stephanie. But he only gets an answering machine. He leaves a message but does not get an answer. "Sophie, we will go ahead and prepare dinner. Maybe they got the message and will be here," he says with a puzzled look on his face.

"Okay, Barth, I have the steaks thawing now," I reply.

"Are we going to have company?" Calah asks.

"Yes, sweetheart, we are going to have your grandfather over," I say.

"Your Dad's father," I continue to explain.

"Donut, we got a grandfather," Calah whispers into Donut's ear as she holds her in her arms. Donut just yawns, as if to say, "Got any more surprises?" She definitely is a cat with an attitude.

"Calah, you want to help me prepare dinner for our company?" I ask.

"Oh, yes, what can I do?" she asks.

I pull the chair over to the sink and run some water into a large bowl. "Stand up on this chair. Here's the strawberries. They need washing. Then I will cut them, and sprinkle a little sugar on them for our desert. We can place them in the refrigerator until later," I say, looking over at an eager little girl, ready to help. We next place the potatoes in the oven for baking. Barth prepares the grill for the steaks. All that is left is the salad, and that is easy to prepare and place into the refrigerator.

Barth didn't give his Dad a specific time to show up, just whenever they could make it. This is alright, especially since it's family. Everything's ready and we are just waiting. Calah's in the bedroom, with Donut and buttons, playing. She has made our bedroom her play area since she doesn't have her own room, right now. I really need to get her some toys to play with since we have not picked anything up from Granny's apartment for her yet.

"Calah, come here for a second," I call.

"Okay, here I come," she yells from the bedroom.

"What kind of toys do you have at your other apartment?" I ask.

"I only have a rag doll, and some dishes. And my table and chairs," she says.

"Barth and I will pick it up for you as soon as we can, and bring it here," I say.

"Then Donut, Buttons and Anne and me we can all have a tea party. You and Barth can have tea with us too. One big family!" She proclaims. I nod my head yes, and smile at Barth.

Hearing the doorbell ring, I walk to the door. Opening the door, John is there. "Hello, Sophie, good to see you guys," he says as he gives me a hug.

Barth walks over, grabbing his Dad's hand. "How are you Dad?" He asks.

"I am good," he replies as he hands me the flowers he's holding in his other hand.

"Oh, thank you," I say. "I will need to get them into a vase of water," I add.

As I leave the room to find a vase to put the flowers into, Calah comes running from the bedroom, but stops short, beside the couch, hugging close to the couch. She's showing a bashful side, that neither, Barth nor I, have seen before. John is a stranger that she's never met, so she feels a little shy with him.

"It's okay, honey," Barth says. "Come over here. I have someone I want you to meet. This is your grandfather," Barth tells her.

Quite the look of surprise comes to John's face. Barth pats him on the back, saying, "Come in and sit down, Dad. We'll explain everything to you."

When his dad had settled in on the couch, Barth began to explain, "Dad, I went out with a girl, when I was right out of high school. Her name was Marsha. It happened before college started. Everyone was invited to a party one of the guys was having at his house. His parents weren't there and there was beer. I'm not making excuses," Barth assures him; then continues, admitting, "Calah.... Calah was conceived. I never knew, honestly, not until a couple of weeks ago."

"Calah, can you help me in the kitchen?" I ask, hoping to get her to the kitchen, so Barth and his father can talk more openly.

"Can I put the plates on the table?" She asks.

"Yes, that sounds good. Come on and Dad and grandpa can talk," I say.

Watching Calah and Sophie leave the room, Barth continued to explain to his dad, "You see, Marsha was killed in a car wreck somewhere out of town. Vera Johnson, her grandmother.....She passed away two weeks ago with pancreatic cancer. Before she died, she told me about Calah... that she is my little girl."

"Barth, did you have a D.N.A. check?" John asks his son.

"I had planned to, Dad," Barth replies. "But, she needs me! I have become so attached to her. It does not really matter! I am her father. I know that I am her father. I don't need a test to tell me. She has been through too much now."

"Son, calm down. It certainly doesn't matter to me. If you say she is your daughter, then she is your daughter!" Barth's father says, reassuring his son. "You know she does look like your mother. I saw it the minute I looked at her," John admits.

"Calah, go tell the guys that dinner is ready," I say.

"Okay," Calah says, as she runs into the living room to inform the guys. "Sophie said dinner is ready. You guys come to the kitchen," Calah says.

"Here we come," Barth says, as he chases her back to the kitchen, with John trailing behind.

John pulls the chair out for Calah. "You want to sit next to me, young lady?" He asks.

"Are you going to be my grandfather?" Calah asks, looking at John.

"I would love to be your grandfather. I have never seen a little girl as pretty as you before," he tells her.

"Donut is a girl cat. Can she be your granddaughter also? She's my new friend," Calah tells him with a bright smile.

"Well... no one can be the same as you, so Donut can be my friend, and you can be my granddaughter. How, about that?"

"Alright, you can come to my tea party. When we get my table and chairs here at my new place."

"Sounds good, Ms. Calah, I will be here," John answers.

Donut takes a look into the kitchen. She is just checking out the new voice. You could almost hear her say, "I was praying that it was not another child. Think I will go back to my favorite place, the bedroom." "Meow!" That was, "I don't need a grandfather, and I am not real sure about the friend business either." Then she disappears.

"Dad, did you ever hear from Steven or Stephanie?"

"No, Barth I have not seen them for a while," he replies.

"I wonder what's up with them. I called and left a message, but I didn't get an answer," Barth says.

"Oh, he's probably just busy. Try to call him again, later," John says. "And I will try also."

Chapter Seventeen

Aware of the phone call from Barth, Steven was busy and could not call Barth back. He had gone home and Stephanie was not there. Steven waited for a while thinking that Stephanie had gone to the store or something, but she did not return. While he was waiting for Stephanie at their house., the phone rang.

"Hello," he answered.

"You do not know me. I know you, and the rest of your family," a mysterious voice said.

"Listen to me, you bastard. Who is this? What do you want?!" Steven asked.

"You got some of my men, and you may have killed Parker. I don't give a damn about them!" The voice tells him. "The drugs that you are holding as evidence, they are worth a good million dollars, and then some. Return the drugs. Don't let anyone else know about this call," the caller said. "And your pretty little wife will be returned!"

"Don't you hurt Stephanie! I will *find you* and *kill you*!" Steven shouted.

"If you want her in one piece, then do as I say."

"Okay, just tell me what you want!" Steven yelled.

"The empty building that you were checking out the other day. I was the street person you were looking for. Bring the drugs there in two days! Bring them at ten o'clock that morning, on the second day."

"How am I suppose to get the drugs? They are monitored closely, until the trial is over." Steven truthfully revealed.

"You will figure out a way!" The voice said and then the phone went dead.

Steven just sat there for a while trying to decide what to do, wondering where this man had Stephanie, and if she was alright. He had been suspicious from the start that the man they had been following was connected to the ring of crooks picked up and arrested at the boat. He knew that he could not tell Barth about any of this. Barth would be right in the middle, trying to get the "Son Of A Bitch!" He did not need the stress, not after what he had been through.

The phone began to ring again. Steven picked it up right away, thinking it was the caller again. "Hello!"

"Steven, what are you doing? I have been trying to get a hold of you for a while," Barth says. "We had Dad over for dinner tonight. We wanted to invite you and Stephanie over also, but I couldn't get you. Where to hell you been these days?" Barth asked.

"Just busy, Barth, you know on domestic cases, a few break ins, nothing major, right now," Steven answered, hoping Barth would accept the answer.

"Maybe we can catch you and Stephanie, the next time."

"Sure that sounds good, Barth," Steven answered.

"Alright, I will catch you later."

"Bye, see you later," Steven said.

After hanging the phone up, Barth looks over at his Dad, who is still at the apartment. I hear him say, "Dad, I tell you something is going on with Stephanie and Steven." Not knowing what the problem could be, he adds, "I will get to the bottom of it."

"Don't you worry about it, Barth," John says.

I sit holding Calah on my lap, with her stuffed Buttons in her hand, nearly asleep, as we watch television after dinner. "I wonder what's going on," I say.

Barth, just shakes his head, with a worried look on his face.

"Well, I am going to have to be going," John says as he stands up. He leans over and kisses Calah on the forehead. She's sound asleep at this point. "Thank you, for a great dinner, Sophie. I feel I ate more than my part." he says as he rubs his stomach.

"I was happy that you came," I say.

"I will be back, to visit with that sweet child," he says, smiling.

"Goodnight, Dad," Barth says as he walks his Dad to the door.

Steven decided to wait until night came to go to the station to slip the drugs out. He was hoping that less people would be there, and he could get them out without anyone seeing him. They were holding the drugs as evidence, until the trial was over, then they would be destroyed.

As Steven entered the building, one of his fellow officers passed him. "Hi, Steven, what are you doing here tonight?" He asked. His name was Frank Brown, an older officer that worked with John more than Steven. He was always friendly and polite.

"Oh, I just had some papers I needed from the office upstairs," Steven replied as he stepped over to the elevators.

"I know how you Cummings are. You work all hours, Just like that father of yours," Frank said as he smiled and walked off.

The elevator ride, up two flights, seemed to take forever. Steven could feel the beads of sweat, across his forehead, running down his nose, as he wiped it away with his hand. He could not help thinking about Stephanie, where she was at and if the creep had hurt her or not. The door finally opened as the elevator came to a stop.

Looking from right to left, making sure he was not being watched, Steven stepped out of the elevator. Doors were all down the long hallway. The room where the drugs were was locked tight. But Steven knew where the keys were kept. He just had to break into that room.

He worked and worked with the door, but it would not open. Finally, he found a piece of strong wire, placed it into the lock, and turned it several times and the door came open. The small cabinet, where the keys to the other rooms are, was not locked. He was in luck, so he grabbed the keys, and ran to the door where the drugs were. Trying every key until finally the right one was used, and the door finally came open.

There were the drugs, on the large table, several large bundles wrapped in white paper. A large postal bag hung on the wall. Quickly grabbing the drugs, Steven placed them into the postal bag, Steven locked the door, and took the keys back to the other room, locking that door. Running back to the elevators, he knew that he had to get out of the building, without Frank or any one seeing him. The bag was heavy and awkward. He was close to the back door and decided to go out this way. No one was around. Most of the officers working tonight were out on their beats, thank goodness for that. He made it to his car that was parked along the side of the building, and placed the bag into the trunk of the car.

Steven's cell phone began to ring. He scrambled to get it out of his pocket, saying frantically, "Yes! Hello!"

"I am watching you. Did you get the Heroin and Cocaine? All of it?" The voice asked.

"Yes. I want to talk to Stephanie!" Steven yelled.

"In time, I will let her speak to you, just not right now," the caller replied.

"You had better not hurt her, I am telling you. I will dump this shit, you will never see it again!" Steven screamed at the caller.

"Just, keep this to yourself, do as you're told, and your little wife will be fine," the caller said and hung up again.

"Damn!" Steven shouted as he hit the steering wheel on the squad car. Then he drove back to his house, waiting the delivery to the vacant building tomorrow morning at ten o'clock.

Chapter Eighteen

Barth and I had retired to bed. Barth is a little anxious about returning to work tomorrow. "Sophie, are you asleep?" He asks as we lie in the bed. Calah is sleeping on the couch with Donut and Buttons. She has gotten used to her new sleeping arrangements, and is sleeping through the night now without any problem.

"No, I am not asleep, Barth," I reply. "Is something wrong?" I ask.

"I was thinking about going back to work.... and Steven...... he is on my mind also. I feel something is wrong," Barth tells me.

"Barth, why don't you get with your Dad tomorrow morning, and the two of you see if you can locate Steven?" I ask. John has been Chief of the Police Department, for the last six years.

"I think I will do that, Sophie. Goodnight. I love you," he says, as he kisses me.

I can't sleep either. I'm thinking about returning to work also. I need to get Calah in a daycare program until school starts again. My studies are finished at the University, but the Boards are coming up and I can't start my own practice until I pass the Boards. Mr. Finch has offered me joining the firm where I work. I probably will take him up on it. My eyes are feeling heavy, and I know that I need to get some sleep.

Steven had stayed up all the night, watching the clock, pacing the floor wondering if he had done the right thing. Stephanie's safe being was all that mattered. He was sure that someone would notice that the drugs were missing today, as he looked at them in the bag sitting in his house, on his floor. "Tick! Tock! Tick! Tock!" the clock counted as the time got closer. It was nine o'clock. He knew that he would have to leave in order to get there by ten o'clock.

When Barth woke up the next morning, he took a shower and dressed. Fixing himself a quick cup of coffee, he went to tell Sophie that he was leaving for work. "Sophie, Sophie," he whispered, trying not to wake up Calah, who is still asleep on the couch. "Honey, I have to be leaving. I will see you tonight," he says.

I turn over and stretch, still tired from not sleeping the night before. "I meant to get up with you. I am sorry, Barth."

"It's okay. You don't have to get up. I will see you later. I love you," he says as he gives me a kiss.

"Okay, bye," I say as I turn over and go back to sleep.

Barth turned into the parking garage at work. Seeing his father's car, he knew that he was working today. He quickly got out of the car, and took the elevator up to the station. Frank was coming down the hall. "Frank, have you seen Dad today?" Barth asked.

"Yes, he's in the evidence room, logging the inventory for the upcoming trials, with the new guy."

"Okay, thanks, Frank," Barth said.

"You bet," Frank answered.

Barth took the elevator up to the evidence room. "What the hell!" He heard John yell.

Barth entered the room. "Dad, is something wrong?" Barth asked.

"All of the damn drugs. They're all gone!" John screams.

The new guy stood scared stiff, not saying a word, not knowing what could have happened to the drugs.

"It's only a million dollars' worth of drugs, and a hell of a lot of evidence to hang on to all the other crimes those crooks committed. Someone's ass has had it!" John yells.

As John and Barth were leaving the room to file a report, Barth hit something with his foot. It went across the floor. Barth leaned over to see what it is. He picked up a ring, reading the inscription, to Steven Cummings.

"Dad, I just stepped on this ring. It has Steven's name inscribed inside," Barth said.

"Let me see that," John said. Looking at the ring, he looked very puzzled. "Barth, don't mention this to anyone else!" John said, looking over at Barth, hoping that the new guy didn't hear the conversation, since the door had closed and he was in the evidence room. "Barth, come with me to the car. We need to find Steven and ask him if he knows anything about this," John said.

John and Barth left the station, on foot, headed to the car, not mentioning anything about the missing drugs, or Steven, to Frank or anyone else at the Police station. There was silence in the car, for a while, until Barth said, "Dad, you know that Steven would not steal the drugs. Don't, you?"

"Of course, I know that! I know if he did, it's because something is threatening him, or his family."

When Barth and John reached the unmarked car that John drove, they got in. John climbed in the driver's side, and Barth sat on the passenger's side.

"Dad, did you want me to drive?" Barth asked.

"No, that's alright. I will drive," John answered.

Making a quick trip through the garage and onto the street, John turned the flashing lights on as they entered the streets of New York, knowing that this would give them a better and quicker escape through the busy traffic there.

"Where do you think Steven, would be?" Barth asked.

As John picked up the radio mike, he paged the squad car Steven should have been in. "This is Captain Cummings, calling squad 357, second page, pick up please" Silence.

"He may be out of the car," Barth said.

"He should have his pager with him," John reminded Barth.

"You know how he is. Sometimes he leaves it on the car seat," Barth replied.

"That's the worst thing ever to do. Suppose you need back up? That should stay right with you, you know that, Barth!" John said, thinking like a father would.

As they turned on the street, where the Little Tot's Clothing Store was, they saw Steven's squad car sitting along the side of the street. "Barth, look, isn't that Steven's squad car?" John asked, pointing in that direction.

"Yes! Dad, pull over and park!" Barth yelled.

John pulled over to the side, jumping out of the car, leaving the flashing lights on. Barth jumped out of the other side.

"I don't see Steven anywhere, do you?" John asked.

"That vacant building, over there, let's check it out!" Barth shouted. "I thought I saw him go in there the other day." Barth reached back inside the car and picked up his radio. "This is officer Barth Cummings requesting backup, at 7896 Madison street, an abandoned building, we need backup."

As they approached the doors to the building, both officers had their weapons in hand. Barth threw the door open as far as it would go. Barth quickly checked behind the door, and John slowly slid down the other wall, making sure there would be no surprises along the way.

The old building was dark inside, even though the morning sun was shining outside. Guns pointed straight ahead, slowly checking every corner, before making the turn, they went farther into the building. Voices could be heard from a distance.

John held his finger to his mouth, indicating, no talking, just listen, as they slowly got closer to the sounds. "You Son of A bitch! Here is your damn drugs! Let me see her, where is she?" Steven screamed.

John and Barth could hear Steven's voice.

"You, Cummings, have hurt my family enough! I am going to kill you!" The dirty, bearded man said, as he pulled out a gun and aimed it at Steven.

By this time, John had turned the corner and was in full view of the man pointing the gun at Steven. "N.Y.P.D.! Drop that gun!" John shouted.

The man remained holding the gun, aimed straight at Steven's head. Shooting nine times, John emptied his gun, making sure the man could not get a shot into Steven. Barth was right behind his father, seeing that John had gotten the crook as he fell to the ground.

"NO...O...O..O!" Steven yelled as he ran to the man on the floor, clinging onto life, as blood ran out the corner of his mouth! "Tell me where Stephanie is. Don't you die! Where is she, tell me!" Steven said as he shook the man.

Chapter Nineteen

Calah and I wake up and have breakfast. I need to get her signed up for a daycare, so I can go back to work in a couple of days. We have a busy day planned, not realizing, what is unfolding with the guys in our lives.

"Calah, we need to get a bath, and get dressed," I remind her.

"But, Donut and I are having fun." She pouts.

"We won't be gone long. You can play when we get back," I say.

"Okay, I will be there in a minute," she says.

I finish in the kitchen, and walk toward the bedroom. "Let's pick out something for you to wear today."

"I want to wear the yellow shorts outfit we bought!" she shrieks.

I Lay out her clothes, as she jumps into the bath. Donut sits on the floor in the bathroom, watching Calah take her bath, wondering, "Why would anyone want to get in all of that water!"

The phone begins to ring. "Hello, I say as I step out of the bathroom, leaving the door open so I can keep a close watch on Calah in the tub.

"Sophie, this is Mom, how are you guys doing?"

"We are doing great!" I answer.

"Your Dad and I are planning to visit New York. We have a chance to go to the Belmont Stakes. Our favorite horse is running for the Triple Crown," Mom says. "I thought we would visit you and Barth. Are we any closer to wedding plans?" She asks.

"Yes, things are looking up. Barth went back to work today," I answer. "Maybe we can set a date," I add. "I haven't heard from Barth yet today. I will tell him you and Dad are coming. I know he will be happy to see you. When are you coming?" I ask. "

"Next weekend," Mom answers.

"Mom, Calah is living with us now. Her grandmother passed away....... and Calah...she needed us," I say.

"That is good, Sophie. I mean, I am sorry for her grandmother to pass, but she needs to be with her father. Does she... does she know about Barth?"

"Yes. He could not stand for her to call him, Mr. Barth." Mom kind of laughed. "Anyway, he told her that he was her father," I explain. I can hear Calah crying from the bathroom. "Mom, I have to go. I have Calah in the bathtub. She is crying. I will see you all next weekend. Okay?"

"Sure, honey, see you," she answers as we hang the phones up.

"Calah! Calah! What is wrong?" I ask as I walk into the bathroom.

"Donut scratched , me!" She cries.

I look at Donut sitting on the floor. She's licking water off of her fur, still wearing a small pile of soap, on top of her head. When she notices that I am looking in her direction, she makes a run for the bathroom doorway for a quick exit. As she takes a fast look back into the bathroom, it is as if she's saying, "What can I say? I went into the survival mode, when the kid included me in bath time."

"Calah, you didn't happen to put Donut in the water, did, you?" I ask.

She has a large cup in the bathtub that she likes to pour the water out of. She plays with this each time she takes a bath. "Donut was in her little boat, and it turned over. She scratched my leg when she jumped out of the bathtub," she tells me.

"Well, we have to remember Donut gets afraid when she gets into water," I remind her. "Let me help you out and I will clean the scratch, put some medicine on it and get you a happy face band-aid. How about that?" I ask.

"Happy face band-aids make the hurt go away, don't they?" She asks.

"Always worked for me," I answer.

Steven leaned over, trying to hear the last words from the dying man, so he could find Stephanie. "I wanted to hurt your family...you killed Parker, my son...the drugs was his..."

"Where is Stephanie? Where is she?" Steven screamed, afraid that the words he needed to hear would not come.

"She has three hours of oxygen... She's at Bergen, Stone Manor road... a grave...." He gasped out the words, trying to mend his ways at the sight of his own ending. Blood bubbled in his throat, as he struggled for the last breath.....and expired.

The backup officers had made it at the scene, as Steven, Barth, and John, jumped into the car to search for Stephanie before it was too late. With siren and lights flashing, they quickly passed car after car.

Bergen was about an hour from New York City, a small country area. But Stone Manor Road was long and winding, a lot of area to bury a person. "Steven, why in the hell didn't you tell us about that creep!" John yelled.

"I couldn't tell anyone. He threatened to kill her and all of you! I did what I thought was the best thing to do!" Steven replied.

"So, he was Parker Brunner's father?" Barth asked.

"He was his father and partner," Steven replied.

"Was he in on the Child abductions also?" John asked.

"I am not for sure," Steven said, very anxious about the time.

"We should be at Bergen in about five more minutes," John said.

Speeding down the road, going about Ninety miles an hour, sirens and lights on, a concrete truck pulled right across in front of the unmarked police car. John's foot hit the brakes, throwing the car into a spin. "That son of a bitch! I should give him a ticket," John said. "Get that license number as we pass by. I will get him later," he said as the concrete driver sat there frozen, knowing very well that he had just pulled in front of a police car.

Barth got the number, as they passed and called it in for the police in this area to follow up on. He also asked if some of the department could meet them at Bergen, on Stone manor, to get Stephanie freed from the grave.

They finally made it to Bergen. There were about fifteen roads before they would reach Stone Manor Road. Steven was not sure what condition Stephanie would be in. She had been in the grave site for two days. Steven realized something was wrong when Stephanie did not return home night before last. He thought that the man probably put her in that grave as soon as he took her.

"I can't remember if I told her that I loved her before I went to work, that day," Steven said, thinking out loud.

"Steven, she is going to be alright. We will find her. She is going to be alright," Barth said to his brother, knowing how he would feel if that was Sophie. He hoped his words helped give Steven some hope.

Steven was about four years older than Barth. He and Stephanie were married right out of high school. Steven joined the police academy, right away, and took some college courses offered through the police department. He always admired his Dad and his career. After their Mom passed away, John raised the boys.

"This is Stone Manor," John said. "Keep your eyes peeled for what looks like fresh dug dirt, or a grave," he instructed.

Barth and Steven looked from right to left, not seeing anything that looked freshly dug, not any fresh dirt anywhere could be seen.

"Turn around; let's go back down the road again!" Steven said helplessly. "Where to hell is it? A dying man would not lie!" He said.

"We don't know what kind of man he was," Barth said, thinking what kind of person would even think about doing such a thing to another person. "He had to be a sick ass!" Barth said, not thinking of how it might make Steven feel. The words just blurted out.

"You got that right," John mumbled.

"Stop! Stop!" Steven yelled. "Over, there! Over, there!"

"Where, Where?" John shouted.

"By that old barn! I see something!" Steven shrieked.

John pulled the car over to the side of the road. The three of them ran to the old barn. As Barth glanced back, he could see cars with flashing red and blue lights, pulling over to the side of John's car and parking also.

"Oh, my God!" Barth yelled. "Dad, Steven, look around, there are at least ten graves here."

"Oh! No!" Steven screamed.

"Steven look! Here! Here is a new one! Here's an oxygen tank. The damn thing is empty. Start digging, quick, start digging," Barth screamed.

Steven started digging with anything he can dig with. Barth, John, and Steven dug as fast as they could, with their hands and an old piece of tin that was on the ground. The other officers came running across the field. They had shovels. They dug and dug, to the bottom of the pipe that was connected to the tank at the top of the ground. There was a wooden box. The officers broke the side of the box. Stephanie was in the box, her hands tied behind her back, and duct tape across her mouth.

"She's not breathing," Steven shouted. "She's not breathing!" Pulling her limp body from the hole in the ground, he quickly pulled the tape from her mouth. Pinching the nostrils together, he gave two breaths, feeling for a pulse....No pulse!

Barth started chest compressions to fifteen, two breaths... chest, compressions to fifteen.... Stephanie gasped for air. Then she began to breath. Steven picked her up into his arms as he began to run to the car. John ran along behind him. "We have to get her to the hospital!" Steven yelled, as an ambulance pulled up next to the police cars at the road.

Steven jumped into the ambulance beside Stephanie, as the E.M.S. person placed the nasal canella to her nose to deliver the oxygen. She had begun to wake up as her eyes searched for Steven. "I am here, baby, I am right here," Steven said, holding her hand tightly, as the ambulance, turned on the siren, and their lights, and headed for the hospital.

Barth and John stayed at the site, to help dig up the other graves. The other graves had skeletal remains of children from ages of five to about thirteen years old. The graves were several years old. Talking to the other officers, John explained, "There will be an investigation to see if this was the man's land, that was killed, or just who it belonged to.

By this time all the news media was surrounding the farm. They all wanted to interview, John, and Barth, and some of the other officers at the site. "Chief Cummings, can you explain what went on here today?" One reporter, from a local news Station asked.

"There will be a report later after we find out more information," John replied. "We do know that we have found skeletal remains from missing children. When we know who these children are, we will let everyone know," he said, trying hard not to bring Steven into the picture just now.

Away from the reports and back to the bodies, Barth said to his father, "When we find out the truth, we will know the man's name. These children, some are showing that they were beat before they died. One had his skull fractured, you can plainly see," he said, as he pointed it out to John.

"Parker could have been an abused child, if that was his father, and did this sort of thing all of his life," John speculated.

"You know they say if you grow up being abused, you often become an abuser also," Barth said, scratching his head, as he looked over all the skeletal remains, which they had dug up.

John heard his radio, "Chief Cummings, we did a search on that land. It belonged to a Norman Hicks. Hicks didn't have any children, and he was never married. The body in the morgue, picked up at the abandoned building at 7896 Madison Street, was Norman Hicks," The dispatcher reported.

"His name was Norman Hicks. He lied about Parker being his son. He never had any children," John said, looking over at Barth. "Thanks. Inform us if any new information appears," John reminded the dispatcher, before ending the conversation.

Calah and I decide to go to Daycares, and check them out today. "Calah, do you want to go to the ice cream parlor?" I ask as I drive down the street.

"I like chocolate; it's my favorite!" Calah says, very excited that we are going to get ice cream.

"Do you like it in a cone, or a cup?" I ask.

"Let's get it in cones," she replies.

As I pull over to Moo, Moo's Creamery, I say, "Calah, you stay in the seat. I will come around to your side and help you out of the car." Calah's side is next to the street. I quickly exit the car and run around to the other side where Calah is sitting. "Hold my hand, the traffic is busy today," I remind her.

"Okay," she says, reaching out for my hand.

I lock the door as we run into the ice cream shop. We walk up to the counter. Signs were everywhere, milkshakes of every kind, banana splits, sundaes, and every kind of ice cream you could ever want.

"What, are we having today?" The lady at the counter asks. She has on a bright pink, stripped dress, a white apron, a small white, banana-shaped hat.

"Chocolate! Chocolate!" yells Calah.

"On a cone honey?" The lady asks with a smile.

"Yes!" answers Calah.

"I bet you would look really cute with one of our hats on. Would you like one? Is it alright, momma?" She asks, looking at me. I nod my head, yes, very proud that she thinks I am Calah's mother.

I pay for our cones, and we find a table to sit at to eat our ice cream. The waitress brings the hat over to Calah. It reads 'Moo, Moo's Creamery' on the side. Calah, very happily, places it on her head and smiles, as a drip of ice cream runs down her chin.

"Here, Calah," I say as I pick up a napkin to catch the chocolate running down her chin, wiping it before it makes its way to her pretty blouse.

The television is on, hanging on the wall. "Breaking News! A man was shot today! He was in an abandoned building, located at 7896 Madison Street. He has been identified as Norman Hicks. No family has been found. They think he had some connection with Parker Brunner, leader of the child abduction ring, that the N.Y.P.D. has been investigating. There will be more news to follow later this evening." They then flashed a picture across the screen of Mr. Hicks.

"Sophie, what's wrong?" Calah asks, as my mouth falls open, and the ice cream I am holding hits the floor. The picture that I'm seeing on the television is...Mr. Hicks...The man I invited into my apartment to spend the day....I thought he was a street person.... I felt sorry for him....I gave him food....He took a shower in my bathroom! These thoughts run over and over in my head. I cannot say anything to Calah. I can't upset her.

"Ma'am, Ma'am," the waitress calls. "Can I get you another ice cream? What flavor? Oh, I remember it was Rocky Road. Can I get you another one?" She asks. "Is everything okay?"

"I am....okay... I finally get the words out. I don't want another ice cream. It's okay. Thank you, anyway."

I sit there with little Calah, trying to remain calm, wondering if Barth was involved in any of this. Today, being his first day back, surely they gave him an easier job, but I know how Barth is, if he can be in the middle of catching a crook he will be there. He's everything it takes to make a great policeman. I suddenly wonder if I can go through life, facing that he might be killed any time. Is that what love is? Loving someone enough to let him be the person he

Linda Givans

wants to be, even if he dies doing it? You, give him all the love you have as long as you have him, and let go when the times comes.

"I am finished with my ice cream," Calah says, taking me away from my thoughts.

"Okay, sweetheart, we can go back to the apartment," I say, looking over at her smiling face, showing chocolate all around her mouth. "I think I had better wipe that face, or Donut will lick it all off!" I say as I give her a little tickle on her belly. Calah laughs and we are on our way.

Calah and I drive back to the apartment. I cannot wait to turn the television on to see what the news is saying about the shooting.

"Sophie, I will find Donut, we can play," Calah says as she runs into the bedroom, looking for the little fur ball.

"Okay, Calah. Barth will be home in a little while," I say, thinking that if I say it, it will happen. "We'll have some dinner then," I tell her.

"I am not hungry!" Calah yells back.

"That is okay. We won't eat until later," I remind her.

Quickly turning the television on, the evening news has just begun. "Breaking News of the day! A man was shot in an abandoned building on Madison Street, today. The N.Y.P.D. was on site at the time. Officer Steven Cummings was being threatened. Chief Cummings came upon the site, and repeatedly asked the man to put the gun down. When he refused, Chief Cummings opened fire, shooting the suspect several times, killing the suspect. Officer, Barth Cummings also was at the site at the time of the shooting."

The news lady continued on to say, "The Cummings family has been employed with the New York Police Department for years. The suspect was identified as Norman Hicks. He is believed to be connected with the leader of the child abduction ring Parker Brunner, and the drugs that were found at Belize, on the freight liner. This was an ongoing investigation lead by Officer Barth Cummings with the F.B.I. Also, there are rumors of grave sites found in Bergen, containing skeletal remains of missing children. This land was owned by Norman Hicks also." The news station also reported, "All officers involved, will be on leave, until this investigation is completed. We will be following up on this news later."

My heart sinks over the news, but I feel relieved that, Barth, Steven, or John were not hurt, this time. I can hear the door opening. As I look up, I see Barth coming through the door. "Barth, are you alright. I have been listening to the news," I say. I run over to hold him just for a moment, knowing he is safe in my arms. I never want to let him go.

"Daddy, Daddy!" yells Calah as she runs from the bedroom to greet Barth, as she hears him come in. He just stands there for a while hugging the both of us. I know that I want to be with him, for however long we have, a day, a month, a year. We are a family now, and God, will watch over us. *I need to have a stronger trust in God,* I think.

"Sophie, we need to go to the hospital. Stephanie is in the hospital. Steven and Dad are there with her. I will tell you about it on the way to the hospital," Barth says, as he kisses me and Calah.

We hurry and leave for the hospital. "I don't want to go for a ride again," Calah complains, as she fidgets in the back seat of the car.

"I know you are tired from being out all day, but this is something we need to do," I say. "Just close your eyes and take a nap. We will be back home soon," I promise.

Holding onto Buttons, she closes her eyes, and it isn't but a short while until she's sound asleep. "Barth, you know that we haven't told Steven or Stephanie about Calah yet," I say, as we stop at the stoplight.

"That's right, I forgot," Barth answers. "Well, I will tell him, when the time presents itself. You can stay with Calah in the waiting room and we can take turns visiting Stephanie," Barth says.

Linda Givans

"Okay, that will work," I answer.

Barth has explained about what happened to Stephanie. I cannot believe that Mr. Hicks was such a bad person. "The graves we found, there were fifteen graves, some were from five years back or longer, missing children that were never found," Barth reveals. "I have a book, at my desk, showing children from several states that our missing. The forensic department is trying to match up with some of these children. Hopefully, to bring some kind of closure to those families, who are waiting to hear something."

We finally make it to Roosevelt Hospital. *These people probably know our name by now*, I think. "Calah, honey, we are at the hospital, wake up," I say.

"Okay, I am awake," she says, stretching, as Buttons drops to the floor of the car. She quickly picks Buttons up. We make our way up to the floor where Stephanie is, after asking at the information desk which room Stephanie Cummings is in. Calah and I sit in the waiting room, as Barth makes his way to room 460.

Barth comes out after a while. "She's going to be alright. She's weak and dehydrated, but they are giving her IV fluids. Steven and Dad are in the room with her," Barth says. "Where is Calah!" He, asks, looking to the empty chair next to me.

"I don't know, Barth! She was just here a minute ago!" I reply as I look down the hallway going to Stephanie's room. Buttons is lying on the floor just in front of the room. Picking Buttons up from the floor, Barth and I run into the room. There stands Calah holding onto John's hand looking at Stephanie.

"Who are you, pretty little girl?" We can hear Stephanie ask, softly.

"Calah! And this is my grandfather!" She answers. "And he needs to come home with me," she adds.

"Your grandfather?" Stephanie and Steven both say at the same time, as Barth and I stand by the doorway with Buttons in my hand.

"I think the time has presented itself," Barth says, as he looks at me and smiles.

The End.